The Immortal Witness

By, Matt Stone

To My Wife.
I Love You
Thank You For All of Your Support.
Lava Lamp

Contents

Trigger Warning:
This story involves some of the greatest evils that
humanity has created and still perpetuates.
Here, I have brought them to light
so that positive progress may forever continue.

I have now died more times than I can remember, and it sucks.

I have been many people and have witnessed many things.

Some of them glorious, *most* of them horrific.

Time and time again, I have been sent forth as *the* messenger, *the* prophet, *the* light bringer, and *the* messiah. Whatever you want to call it, that's me. I am the only consistent product of the Earth, and in one form or another, I have been ever-present. That is, ever-present, and ever-opposed by the very darkness within all humans, the darkness that I myself am tasked with healing.

I was the Buddha; I was Jesus. I was Muhammad. I was Harriet Tubman. I was Martin Luther King Jr., I was Gandhi. I was Helen Keller, and I was Mister Rogers. These are some of the most notable. Even against great odds, I was afforded the right times, locations, and circumstances, to be able to positively affect as many people as possible.

But, every single time, I had to fight and struggle against the human race to make my voice heard. And even after I had made headway, my words were greatly altered by humankind, whether by accident with translation, or on purpose by those seeking more wealth. Hell, notoriety didn't even come until after I died, the putzes then using my words to enslave and empower.

This is my purpose. I *am* kindness and compassion, confronting anger and indifference. I *am* love and selflessness, facing down hate and greed. I *am* knowledge and comprehension, in constant contention with the rebuke of science and the championing of ignorance. I am *all* of us, as a part of each has been a part of me, and I have now been all but lost amid humanity's hubris.

I am the embodiment of our global consciousness, yet humans have decided otherwise. I am the messenger that is to share the manner in which people operate most optimally, in attempts to maintain the symbiosis of *the whole*: Jehovah, Earth, God, Yahweh, Gaia. But humanity increasingly chooses to place themselves above all else, even at their own peril. My mission is to trudge the mortal waters, and provide the best example of living for human beings, in hopes that we all may become the most positive influences possible. But again and again, my messages have been bastardized and used for control and personal gain. Frankly, it's really starting to fucking piss me off.

Becoming as influential as I was when I was Jesus is not easy. More often than not, I die having only been able to share my message with those closest to me; sometimes no one at all. Lives upon lives have been met with violence and hate, and eons have passed as I've struggled. I am forever plagued by the very-human forces of avarice, antagonism, and oppression that continually block my path. For every life of mine that is enshrined in history, there are millions more that have slipped unnoticed through the ignorant cracks of humanity.

After so many years, so many lives, and so many deaths, I can feel my righteous indignation growing.

*

My human embodiments are not aware of their destined fates until they are physically capable of hosting my being. After the particular child or teen has experienced enough of the world to be ready, we merge. I am made whole again in my corporeal being, and can attempt to further my mission.

For humans, it may almost seem fun to be able to return to youth time after time, and it very well can be. But the downside is getting thrown into the roulette wheel of varying childhood circumstance. I never knew what family I would show up in, their economic standings, or even their religious beliefs. In one life I could have every possible monetary resource at hand, only to be snuffed out by a falling piece of some douchebag's homemade jetpack. Then in the next life, I could arrive in a family of the poorest of the poor, maybe able to access a vast audience of eager believers, but have only a modicum of impact before passing away from some preventable disease. There was always *something*…

It is not all doom and gloom though. I am at peace during my stay in what I think of as our "energy pool" between lives. This is my time to reflect upon my past life. After a while, my soul regathers itself, and I am reborn to proceed with my mission once again. I am constantly present, and am always accounted for within *the whole* of Earth.

*

I have currently been here in the great pool for some time after a long life as a musician. I was feeling fairly good (for once) about having been able to implement some vast changes with this life. I was able to share my words with millions of people in a way that will be remembered for a relatively long time by human standards, and I have always enjoyed living as a musician. This particular one will forever rest among the stardust.

Even though I had been there for a while, I was still feeling the high of my accomplishment when I got the first inklings of the duty. My reformation begins with human hunger. A growing, insatiable need for the food of the Earth, that not only reminds me of my upcoming duty, but also of my deep physical connection to *the whole*. The hunger rumbled, and it was time again to try to change the world forever.

This was different though. Whenever my next tour of duty will be monumental, I can tell. There is a bit more energy provided for my new start, an alternate sensation to the beginning… a buzz. It is rare that I have such a powerful influence twice in a row, but… this feels *really* different.

In long wisps of pure kindness, my bits and pieces were rallied from the reaches of the pool, "Us" as it was etched into my deepest existence. I became complete, and I was whisked off again to shove my messages of love and compassion into evil's mealy mouth.

Chapter 1

It was December, and I'm really glad that I remembered to grab a coat as I rushed out of the house.

I could see my breath when I stepped onto the porch, and my hand left trails on the railing in the frost as I went down the front steps. It was way too early for me to have left for school, but given the argument with my mother that had just taken place, I really needed to not be there. That's how the dawn found me wandering the streets of the big city; the empty streets seemed to help my mood. The huge buildings blocked the rising sun, but it wasn't freezing anymore. It rarely iced over in this city; even more rare was snow, so it had that going for it. I always hated it when I had to shovel the snow before we moved. The lack of snow was at least something.

My phone still worked as an MP3 player, so I was able to listen to my music as I passed by shop owners while they swept and sprayed down their portion of the sidewalk for the start of their day. Delivery trucks were unloading their morning goods to local restaurants. Taxicabs sat idling outside the fancy hotels while they waited for their fares to appear. A few people still mingled around the twenty-four-hour pizza shop after a long night of drinking. My soundtrack was my lo-fi mix as I watched the homeless encampments begin to stir and shake the cold dew from their shelters. The city was different in the morning. Not really quiet (it was never quiet), but it wasn't so loudly blaring its city self. It was cleaner, maybe. The air didn't reek of pee – much – and there were no sidewalk-clogging tourists out yet. No panhandlers, no peddlers; it was almost calming.

I found myself in the middle of the financial district and I sat down on the edge of a large fountain positioned in front of the headquarters of a major bank. I took off my backpack and unzipped the little pocket on the front. I reached in and took out a small picture that I kept in there. It was of one of my earliest memories, a day trip to the county fair with Mom and Dad when I was four years old.

We had spent six hours that day playing carnival games, eating junk food, and enjoying the rides. I only remember small bits of it, but I *do* remember how happy we were. On the way out, there was an old photo booth that cost five dollars for three of those tiny little pictures that came in a strip. Even Dad wanted his picture taken after such a great day and all three of us packed into the box with huge grins. When we got home, Mom cut the pictures apart and handed them to Dad and me. She told us that days like that didn't happen very often, and that we would always have the strength to look forward to the next one if we kept the last one close to our hearts.

I don't know what they did with theirs, but mine lived in my backpack. Even with a heart so heavy, I smiled as I looked at it. Mom holding the large stuffed banana that Dad had spent twenty dollars to win. Dad smiling like he had just won the lottery, and me sitting on their laps loving every minute.

I became faintly aware of someone coming towards me, and I looked up from the picture to see a homeless woman approaching. Her hair was pointing in every direction, she wore a faded trench coat that almost touched the ground, and she mumbled as she walked. She was pushing a small cart in front of her. It came to a squeaking halt as she pulled it up alongside the fountain.

She began pulling out armfuls of clothing, dirty from the looks of it, and heaped them on the ledge of the fountain, close enough to me for a wayward sock to land on my foot. I kicked it back to the pile, and watched as she started dunking a pair of jeans in the fountain. I jammed the photo back in my bag and got out of there.

I lost track of time. I'd had two hours to get to school when I initially turned my music on, but when I looked at the time, I realized I was down to forty-five minutes. Shoot. I looked around to see where I was and I saw a bus stop a block down. I hurried over, weaving my way through the traffic stopped at the light. I looked over the route map and realized the bus I needed wouldn't be there for another ten minutes. This was going to be a problem because my new city skills were telling me the ride would take around thirty-five minutes, which wouldn't leave me much time to actually get to class. Not that I really wanted to be there anyway.

I sat down on the bench between a man in a business suit and a college student. They both scooted over to make room. The student looked like she went to art school, judging from the sketch pad under her arm and her pink hair, and also because as I sat down, I could smell what she had been smoking for breakfast. Nobody said anything. We were just a few people trying to get our day started and enjoying the silence.

The bus came and I crowded on with the others and found a seat in the back. I checked my phone. I *was* going to be late again, *and* my battery was going to die soon. I turned off my cell and put my earphones in my pocket. The bus lurched forward as soon as the doors closed and it pulled sharply into traffic. With no music, I resigned myself to staring out of the window.

The towering buildings still struck me as odd and affronting. I had not grown up in such an environment, far from it, and these huge monuments of business seemed to mar all that I had come to hold dear. My dad had been born to a farming family upstate, where they owned large orchards of almond trees. It was there that the family "kept its heart in the soil." For generations, we had been cultivating and processing nuts that were shipped country wide. The family had been on the farm for over a hundred years and it was in their blood. It was in *my* blood.

Grandpa had died of a heart attack before I was born, and my dad had to quit school to come back home and run the farm. He was nineteen then, had barely left home, and he was saddened to have to return so soon. Young, and a bit ignorant of the world, Dad did his best. He had paid close attention to his own father so he knew what he was doing. He was even one of the first nut companies to be on the internet. He not only took over his father's legacy, but also grew the small family farm. Of course, the dream was for me to take over when it came time.

I too grew up on the farm. I followed my father around incessantly as a child, and I absorbed all I could from him. I learned how to trim the trees, and how to set up the irrigation. I sat on his lap and drove the tractor as we hauled branches to the burn piles, and I could trap a ground squirrel with the best of them.

Most importantly, he taught me what his own father had taught him. Dad spoke to me of the balance that he maintained with the Earth. He didn't see his work as a one-sided deal. He had to work in tandem with the forces of nature, a give-and-take, so that the high level of respect could be maintained. This provided an order for all involved to be able to succeed, trees and humans alike.

On our farm, Dad told me that it was the almond blossoms. The level of respect we paid to the blossoms was evident every spring when the blossoms appeared for our orchard's regeneration. After each winter, our rows and rows of trees would explode in the pinks and whites of new life. Dad could spot troubled trees by the way their flowers grew. Not enough water, not enough fertilizer, not pruned properly, soil pH off; he swore he could tell all of this through the blossoms and their differing hues.

I never knew if he was kidding or not, but I used to love the spring when our trees had flowers on them. This was my own personal magical realm, a realm that smelled of honey. It was exactly like in the movies or comics, when a cherry orchard in full blossom continuously rains petals down on a pair of lovers, or dueling swords-people, and the ground seems covered in pink and white snow.

I would climb through the branches and wage epic wars with my GI Joes while Dad fixed a broken pipe or checked the squirrel traps. I would swing from the branches to make the petals fall quicker, and I would run as fast as I could to watch the flowers rise from the ground in my wake. I had been happy in the early days of my childhood. Now I missed my dad… and my happiness.

*

I was snapped out of my memories when the bus's horn blared and we came to a sudden stop. I stood up from my seat to see what was going on, and I shook my head at what I saw. A car had somehow become wedged on the curb at an intersection, and was unable to move. Other cars were attempting to get around it, further blocking other people in. It was becoming a pileup right in front of us... I was starting to panic. I could *not* be late again. I had just begun weighing the option of hopping out the window and making a run for it, when the decision was made for me. One car sped up and attempted to cut in front of us, and I heard the driver yell out the window, "Not today, buddy," as he hit the gas.

I have been surprised by the bus drivers in the city. They take a lot of flak from people who ride the bus, like A LOT, but this tolerance does not extend to humans in cars. Buses ruled these roads. All ways were *their* ways, and today was no different for this driver. Clearly a seasoned veteran, he expertly blared the horn and pulled out in front of the line-cutting hatchback, then began expertly maneuvering through the inner-city mayhem. He whipped the wheel back and forth as he dodged one car after another, until in no time, the road ahead of us was clear. They seriously do not pay these people enough.

We were still making great time, but it was certainly going to be close. We hit the bus stop by the school, and I commended my charioteer as I left. I stepped down onto the sidewalk and the doors hissed closed behind me. The bus pulled away and I saw the front of the school across the street. I looked around; there were no other kids around. Class had already started, and I was late again.

The school was relatively new to me, and I hadn't made any friends yet, even after three months. I guess that last part was mostly my fault. I had not made any effort to make new friends. I wasn't ready. I was still a stranger to them, and that's how I liked it. I ate lunch by myself, usually outside if the weather permits, and I have successfully pushed away any cheerful welcome waggoners. I wasn't up for it, not yet. The move had provided me with the opportunity to choose who I was to these people. They didn't know who I used to be, and I have yet to figure out who I am.

Speeding through the school to my locker, I jerked it open. I shoved my backpack inside and grabbed my history and math books. I slammed the locker shut, and my footsteps echoed as I ran down the deserted hallway to Mrs. Cliner's class.

Through the door I could hear her already deeply immersed in the day's lesson. We were continuing our "deep dive" into World War II, something I already knew quite a bit about, and she seemed to be going on about the many countries that had been overrun by the Germans during the war.

I peeked through the window in the door, and saw that she was at the blackboard drawing a timeline of the German conquest. Her back was to the door, her hair bun and knitted sweater facing me, and I hoped she'd stay that way as I eased the doorknob. I crouched as the door opened wide enough for me to squeeze through, and I gently pushed the door closed before letting go of the knob on the other side. Mrs. Cliner didn't turn around, but the other students certainly noticed my attempts at ninja tricks, and they tried to stifle giggles behind their textbooks. The laughter piqued Mrs. Cliner's spidey-sense, and she turned to face the class, just as I sat down in my seat.

She looked at me. "Jacob, thank you for finally gracing us with your presence today," she said. "You will stay after class and speak with me about your continued tardiness; that makes three times this week." I nodded but didn't say anything, and she turned back around to continue with her lecture. I propped my own textbook up on my desk and laid my head down behind it in defeat.

It had been a rough morning, overall. Between the crap before I left, the memory of my childhood, the stressful bus ride, and now having to stay after class, I was tired already. And it was only first period. At least Mrs. Cliner didn't call on me to answer any questions, but there was a quiz at the end of class nobody told me about. I hadn't remembered to grab a pencil from my locker, which Mrs. Cliner pointed out as she handed me the test.

"Jacob, how do you expect to succeed on this test, or in life for that matter, if you don't show up prepared?" she asked me. I mumbled something about having lost it, even though I knew full well that I just wasn't thinking about it at the time.

"Well, you better find one quickly, or you will receive an F on this quiz," she said as she glared at me over her glasses. I could see she was getting frustrated, and I was about to get up and run to my locker to grab one, when the kid sitting next to me turned from his own test with a sigh. He reached into his bag, took out a black case, and retrieved a brand-new yellow number-two pencil. He leaned over and handed it to me across the aisle. I nodded a thank-you as I took it, then turned silently back to my test, ignoring his attempt at a "you're welcome" smile. My frustration and anger wouldn't allow for it; these people were still strangers to me. I was just glad that the pencil was already sharpened so I didn't need to draw further attention to myself.

The quiz was a joke. It was basically a fill in the blank of the significant events of the war. The invasion of Poland, Dunkirk, the capture of Paris, the entrance of the United States, and so on. I already knew all of this. Not only had relatives served and fought during these times, but I had also done my own "deep dive" into all things military after 9/11 when Dad got his own ideas about being Captain America. I had scoffed when I learned that the class only went back to the nineteen-thirties, thinking that it was an extremely small window of history. I felt cheated by the class. I could be actually learning things.

I finished the quiz in record time, and noticed Mrs. Cliner eyeballing me as I put my head back down. I ignored her and attempted to keep from counting the minutes until class ended. Three months in, and I already had detention.

The bell finally rang for the short break in between classes, but I didn't move until I felt all of the other students leave. I rose slowly and picked up my things. I stopped for a moment and thought about returning the dude's pencil to his desk, but then I tucked it into my own empty pencil case instead.

I took my quiz up to Mrs. Cliner's desk to place it atop the pile left by the other students. Her hand shot out and grabbed the quiz before I could release it. She motioned for me to pull up a seat as she reviewed my answers. I noisily dragged a nearby chair over to her desk and plopped down to await my fate.

"Well, you definitely know your history," she said. "You knew these off the top of your head. All of your work, when you turn it in that is, has been full of insight and wisdom. As such, I feel that your overall lackadaisical attitude towards promptness and the attention this class requires may be due to boredom."

My ears perked up as I listened to her describe much of what I had been feeling, minus the really bad parts, of course. But it was starting to sound like I wasn't going to be in trouble. She continued, "I will have to assign you detention for the tardiness. This cannot be helped, but during those three days of after-school detention, you and I can discuss an alternate curriculum that may better keep your mind occupied during my class. In addition, I am aware of the circumstances that have brought you to us, and I have taken these into consideration. But, Jacob, you need to start engaging with your classmates. You have been here for three months now, and everyone needs someone to talk to every once in a while. Make a friend."

She had a way of maintaining her studiousness, while also effectively conveying her concern and leniency. "What alternative curriculums are you proposing?" I asked. "I would like to be fully aware of the details before I agree to any terms of this treaty."

I thought I caught a whisper of a smile pass over her lips before she regained what little composure she had lost and she answered, "There have been many recent archaeological digs that would suggest that our historic concepts of the discovery of the Americas are incorrect. There have been remains found that prove that Vikings were present in North America a thousand years ago, displacing Columbus as the discoverer he is made out to be by five hundred years. I would like to know more on the subject, as well as your thoughts on how this might change the future historical records, as well as what it means for humanity."

Mulling this over, I decided it was a very fair offer. Especially when a more serious punishment could easily be had. Plus, it sounded really interesting. Then, thinking of my day so far, I saw an opportunity. "I will agree to your terms, as long as we can change the after-school detention to before-school."

She responded a bit too quickly for my liking, with "Deal! I get here every day at six a.m. I will require you to be here promptly at six-thirty tomorrow, Thursday, and Friday." With that, she stuck out with her hand to seal the deal. I shook it, nodded at her, and noisily replaced my chair. I promised that I would look into this Viking news of hers, and that I would see her here in the morning.

I had to hurry to get to my next class. I was too occupied by my new mission to pay much attention in Algebra II. The teacher had a tone that sounded like a low-flying crop duster and the excitement to match. He paid no attention to the students, choosing only to present the information, but not ensuring that anyone was engaged in the learning. This led to a motley assortment of activities around the room. Some girls painted their nails in the corner. Others were clustered around their phones, laughing. I did notice the guy who'd given me the pencil sitting in the back of the room actually taking notes.

The last open seat was just behind him, so I headed that way. There was no need to sneak into this class. The teacher couldn't have cared less. I sat down behind pencil-boy. I stared at the back of his head for a bit, and noticed just how small he was. He could have passed for a middle school student, but he was here among us juniors. He was probably supersmart, but I'm sure being here was no picnic for him.

I pulled out my phone and charger, and plugged it into the nearby wall outlet. I had written down the school's Wi-Fi password when I noticed it taped to the principal's desk during my intake, and I had been able to use my phone at school, even when my service was suspended whenever Dad forgot to pay my bill. I began searching for the new findings that Mrs. Cliner had been talking about. Had precursors to Columbus been previously known? It's possible that one of the many museums cover-ups I had recently read about was related, where places that were supposed to be neutral parties of science had long been "losing" artifacts that didn't fit with *certain* narratives.

I was still lost in the possibilities when the lunch bell rang and the teacher finally quit his feeble attempts at furthering the next generation. I left and joined the waves of other students coursing through the halls.

I headed back to my locker and stowed my books. Most of the other students were going to the lunchroom and I followed. My mind was full of the new discoveries I had been reading about, and I was surprised to find myself getting excited about the prospects. I had not been excited in a long time.

I was smiling to myself when I noticed another student walking along the line to find a seat. He was a bigger guy, probably about six feet already, and he didn't look happy. His white T-shirt and jeans were a bit dingy, and his red hair looked like it had never seen a comb. His hands had a death grip on his tray and he was scowling.

As he got nearer to me, I noticed a flash of white coming from his jeans. The guy's fly was open. I probably should have stuck with my troubled silence, but I was feeling good about having a new adventure to look into, and I spoke up without really thinking. "Dude, your fly is open."

I was honestly trying to help him, but that isn't how it went down. He stopped and looked at me like he was trying to figure out who I was. Then he realized what I had said, and he quickly shifted his tray to look down at his pants. Whatever anger had been there was replaced with embarrassment, as he turned bright red and attempted to zip up. He took one hand off his tray and reached down, leaving the tray and its contents awkwardly balanced.

I, and those around us, watched in fascination as his meal started to wobble uncontrollably. He noticed it too, but was stuck with the option of saving his food or saving his dignity, and he chose the latter. His tray tilted towards him, right as he managed to finish adjusting his pants, and lunchroom lasagna, salad, and drink all crashed down his front. The drink, an unopened can of soda, hit the floor between his feet and began spraying its contents straight up into his face. He was smeared with sauce and dressing, a few leafy greens clung to him, and the soda made it look like he had wet himself. He looked around in utter embarrassment as the rest of the students erupted in laughter.

Kids were standing on the tables to better see the mess, and soon, the entire room was one big finger-pointing mortification. I would have laughed too, but the guy got redder than ever, his humiliation turned to anger, and he locked his eyes with me. It looked like he blamed me for the whole thing. I attempted to tell him I was only trying to help, but I couldn't find the words. I was still a bit struck by what had just happened. I could only stammer as the guy pointed directly at me, his eyes glaring, and then made that weird throat-slashing gesture. He turned and ran, leaving the mess and choruses of laughter behind. Great, my first friend was an enemy.

As I got my own food, I saw the janitor headed over with his mop and bucket to clean up the spilled food. It was still cold outside, so I decided to stay inside to eat. I could hear the various conversations about what just happened as I looked for a place by myself, and I noticed that the permutations of the story were already starting.

"The new kid tripped him, and he peed himself!" A group stared at me as I passed. I thought about correcting them, but my mouth had already gotten me in a lot of trouble so far. I sat down at a far corner table and ate my lunch alone. Hushed whispers and pointing continued as I ate, but I kept my head down and watched a video on ancient Viking travel.

I had art class next, which gave me reason to forget the big kid and his lunch. I had been struggling to find something, anything, to sculpt for our project that was coming due. The previous week, we were given five pounds of clay and told we must prepare something to be fired by the end of this week. I hadn't been able to decide what to make with my clay, and now it was Tuesday. I had to have something by Friday.

I was pushing my lump around and hoping the dude didn't really blame me for the accident at lunch, when my lump began to look a bit like a canoe. A bit more working and it started to resemble a long boat. Soon, I had all but forgotten the big guy, and I began attempting to sculpt a Viking sailing vessel. I carefully smoothed the sides and shaped the long form that supposedly had carried the Vikings all the way to a new world.

They were not elaborate ships but were instead plainly made from long stretches of timber, notched, and sealed with resin. The focal point, aside from the large sails that I would have to attach somehow, would be the large head of a sea serpent on the bow. In true Norse fashion, my boat would bring terror to those who witnessed its emergence from the fog.

I spent the rest of the class deeply engrossed in my project, and was a bit sad when I heard the bell ring. I cleaned up, making sure to wash off my tools so that they would be pristine when I returned the next day. I placed the work in my designated cubby, serpent head out, alongside the vase of my cubby partner, careful not to bump either. I headed back through the halls to my locker to get my Economics book for my last class of the day. I kept my head down as I dodged other students, so I didn't see it right away.

It wasn't until I was reaching for my lock to twist in my combo that I noticed someone had hastily scratched the word "deed" into the front of my locker. I stared at it for some time, wondering what the hell it could mean, before some student passed behind me and said, "You're dead, dude."

Oh... That made more sense. My lasagna friend was out for revenge. I just wanted to be left alone. I opened my locker and packed my bag. I took it with me to my next class so I could leave from there. He would probably look for me at my locker after school, and the best plan was to be anywhere else.

Econ dragged. I sat there constantly aware of the ticking clock, prolonging the agony further. I couldn't pay attention to the teacher because I was trying to come up with ways to get out of fighting the other guy. He was a good foot taller than me, and I didn't like my odds. Best to avoid it altogether if I could.

Luckily, my class was in a room that was at the very edge of the school's property, and I could make a dash for public transportation pretty easily. Then it hit me. Even if I was successful at dodging a bully today, I would still eventually have to go home. This day would end badly, one way or another.

I was the first one out of the door, even before the bell stopped ringing. I could hear a stampede behind me as class retired for the day, and the entire high school rushed to get on with their social lives. The noise quieted as I ran around the corner of the building away from everyone. I dashed towards the black protective fence bordering the school.

The fence kept out the wayward street folk and was a deterrent against ditching. But the bars were curved downward at the top and pointed outward to the street. This prevented people from coming in, but not necessarily from getting out.

I cinched my backpack higher and headed to the corner. I had climbed plenty of things in my lifetime: trees, old pump houses, even flagpoles, so scaling a fence like this should be no problem for me. I reached the top easily and was able to slide over the curved part and lower myself down as far as I could for the final eight-foot drop. I landed pretty perfectly, even accounting for the weight of my books in my bag, but my shoe wasn't having it. I hit the ground, and heard a small *pop* that was accompanied by a bolt of pain.

I gathered myself and limped down the sidewalk and around the corner, out of immediate sight of the school, before stopping to examine my ankle. It turned out that the noise had been my shoe. There was a large crack that ran the width of it, and I could see the cloth padding through the split. My ankle must have only been shocked a bit, because it was already starting to feel better.

These weren't expensive shoes by any means, but they were all I had. I tied both shoes a bit tighter, and headed for the bus stop. I didn't aim for the closest stop, but the one after that. That way, if someone was looking for me, I wouldn't be in the most likely place. As I walked, I noticed that my broken shoe could breathe. Cold air was pouring in with every step, and winter had only just begun. I sighed.

A bus pulled up just as I arrived at the stop, and I boarded showing my student ID as fare. The only seat available was next to a little old lady who had a small dog in her purse sitting on her lap. I sat down beside her, and watched her shift the dog so it was facing away from me. I guess my face was broadcasting my dark mood. She changed seats as soon as one became available, fine with me. I stretched out a bit and put on a better scowl to deter others from sitting next to me. I had dodged Big Red from the lunchroom, so that was a positive. I felt like I'd actually made a connection with Mrs. Cliner, so that was a plus too, but I still felt like my life was in shambles.

When the planes hit the World Trade Center, I was only seven years old. I didn't quite understand what the attack meant, but my dad had told me what it meant to him. Soon after the initial shock began to wear off, he took me for a walk in the orchard.

It wasn't springtime, so there were no blossoms, but the trees were still leafy, and some held a few stubborn almonds on their branches. He explained the entire scenario, as we understood it then, and he said that it made him feel a weakness he never wanted to feel again.

The country had built up an overinflated sense of safety, and the attack was a wake-up call for my father. He had spent the majority of his life in isolation, only sharing himself with the land (and me and Mom, of course), but never looking to help with bigger causes. He rarely voted, as he considered many of the politicians to be corrupt. He even stayed away from churches, because to him, they had become more about social standing than worshiping God. He preferred to venerate among God's creations that he personally cared for, his trees. As he put it, this country had been good to him and Dad wanted to give back. The age limit for enlistment was thirty-five at that time, and Dad was well under the line. He told me he would be joining the Army and going to fight the war on terror. He told me that he was going to go and make sure that Mom and I would be safe forever.

Dad hired a few men to do general maintenance around the place, and soon he was on a plane to boot camp. Mom and I cried as we watched the plane take off. I waved a little American flag at the departing plane until it disappeared from sight. Dad finally came back after fourteen long weeks, and he looked like a superhero to me when he surprised us at home earlier than we expected him. He was clean-shaven and they had given him a respectable buzz cut. He was decked out in a full camo uniform with highly polished boots, and he seemed like he had come alive out of my GI Joe collection. Mom welled up with tears as we both jumped up from the table where we were working on my homework; she even knocked over her chair. We ignored it as it clattered to the floor and we raced into Dad's waiting arms.

Dad was only home for two days before he was to ship off on his first deployment. We had picnics, and played all day, and reveled in all that was our family. Those were two of the happiest days of my life.

He left again that Sunday. It was raining as we stood on the porch and watched him give us a final wave as the cab drove off. He promised he would be back in six months, for two weeks, and that we could have picnics in the orchard every day when he returned. I was proud of my dad, who was going to be a hero.

He did come back after six months, but we didn't have any picnics. Dad smiled as we ran to greet him on his return, but that was the last time we saw him happy. He stayed in bed those two weeks and drank. We didn't play catch, he didn't take me for walks, and he wouldn't talk about what happened to him while he was away. It was almost like he hadn't come home. My mom told me to stay away from him at night because he was dealing with grown-up things, but I know now that it was because he was too drunk by then to be trusted with me.

I was scared for him. He didn't seem to be the same person who had left. This wasn't my dad. Something had changed in him and I didn't like it. The two weeks passed quickly, and Dad left again. He wouldn't even let us take him to the airport, opting for a taxi, almost as if he was in a hurry to put us behind him.

This time, he only managed a half wave through the rolled-up window as the car drove away. Mom and I went back into the farmhouse and sat on the couch. I remember her pulling me close to her as she began to sob.

At first, I cried with her. But after a while, I was all cried out. I told Mom that I had to use the bathroom and got up. She lay across the couch and I pulled the blanket from the back down onto her. I could hear her muffled crying, even over the water as I washed my face and brushed my teeth. She hasn't really stopped crying since.

Every time my dad would come back, more of him was gone. Physically, he still seemed to be in his prime, but he was becoming someone different. His contract was only for two years, but those two years took their toll. His yelling got to be so much; it was like he didn't know how to communicate any other way. I played outside mostly, but I could still hear him screaming sometimes, even all the way out in the orchard.

At the end of the two years, we were no closer to winning the fight against terrorism and my dad was gone. When he finally did come home for good, he spent a day fixing up an old shed. He put a busted armchair, a fridge, and a TV inside. He sat in his shed, day after day, yelling at the news about the war.

Years went by. The farm started falling to pieces and I still wasn't really old enough to be of much help. We could no longer pay for work around the place, and Dad didn't seem to care, so we adapted. Mom got a part-time job at the library and I picked up my first job as a paperboy. We made ends meet.

I was returning from my route one spring day when I walked into the house to find silence. Mom was in the laundry room with a pile of towels and her earphones on. I tugged at her sleeve and asked her why I couldn't hear Dad yelling. She turned off her music and looked at me questioningly, before realizing she couldn't hear him either.

She put the towels in a basket and we went to the back porch to see what was going on. We stood there, twenty feet from the old shed, and heard only silence. She looked at me and took me by the hand. We went down the steps and around the little garden Mom had planted.

"Maybe he fell asleep," she whispered, as we neared the door.

It stank. I was thirteen, so I knew enough to recognize the smell as a combination of beer and unwashed human. Mom and I peered into the shed and let our eyes adjust to the darkness. He wasn't here. There were beer cans strewn all over the place, and the chair looked like it was going to fall apart. The TV was sticky from the drinks he had thrown at it, and the foil on the rabbit ears had grown to the size of softballs. It was disgusting, but empty. He couldn't have gone far, because Mom still had the car keys, so we began to walk around the house to see if he had passed out somewhere.

We were circling around the front of the house when something held me back and told me to look towards the orchard. As I turned, about a hundred yards away, I could see a large shape lying next to one of our oldest trees. Its darkness stood out against the sea of springtime "snow."

"Mom," I said slowly, and pointed for her to look. We ran to him. As we got closer, Mom grabbed me to prevent me from getting any closer. She pulled me to her and hugged me, in order to keep me from seeing what Dad had done to himself with Grandpa's old revolver. But I was growing and I was just tall enough to see over Mom's shoulder. I couldn't see everything but I could see the deep stains that spread out, forever marring my childhood blossom kingdom.

I took it better than my mom. Dad had long ceased being the focus of my adoration. He had not only allowed himself to become weak, but his old words about honor and family seemed like complete lies now. Between the war and his drinking, I felt like my dad had died a long time ago. I had already mourned him by the time he actually passed, so I didn't have much left. Mom, on the other hand, was completely broken. He had been her only love for much of her life, at least until I came along, and when Dad took himself, he took much of her too.

*

By this time, I had made it all the way home. The bus ride had been uneventful, which was a blessing, when so many other rides were filled with drunks and druggies causing havoc. I stood on our new porch and noticed that the yard would have to be taken care of before winter really began. The bushes were overgrown and blocking parts of the walkway, the grass had grown to over a foot, and leaves clogged the gutters. Maybe I could borrow some tools from a neighbor or something.

I paused with my hand on the front doorknob. This was my least favorite part of the day. I never knew what I was about to walk into. I opened the door and took off my shoes. I didn't hear the TV on, so it had either shut off when Mom fell asleep, or she had gone out for one of her impromptu "runs." I hung up my jacket and headed to the kitchen. I wasn't hungry. I wanted to see if the source of my morning frustration had been dealt with. It had not, and exactly what I had warned her about had happened. There were still pills strewn across the kitchen, pills that I had asked her to clean up, and she hadn't.

After Dad's death, Mom's best friend Aunt Jackie – who wasn't my real aunt – had given Mom something to help her with her "moods," and that was all it took. Mom became addicted almost instantly, and life continued to go downhill. I despised Aunt Jackie and I told her to stay away from us as soon as I realized what was going on, but she was Mom's dealer, and even if she didn't come to the house, they'd meet somewhere else. Even after we lost the farm and moved to the city into my great-grandparents' old house, Aunt Jackie would make the long drive to meet Mom. Mom had to buy in bulk now, which sometimes led to messes like the one I was staring at.

It wouldn't matter so much if it were just her and me living here. *I* know not to take the pills. But shortly after moving, I had found a helpless stray kitten in the backyard. Mr. Peanut recovered from his outdoor abandonment and he quickly became one of my only sources of joy. Here in front of me, Mr. Peanut lay dead, a pool of pill-riddled vomit in front of him. She had promised me that they would be cleaned up, and she had even made a show of grabbing them and putting them back into their bottle as I went out the door, but whatever. Never trust a junkie with something that you love…

I couldn't take it anymore. I left the cat for Mom to find and ran upstairs to my room. I slammed the door shut and double locked it. I had had to install deadbolts because Mom had started sneaking in at night during her "upper" times, and waking me whenever she felt like having bonding moments. I flung myself onto the bed and pounded my pillow.

We had been forced off our farm. (Not that it had been easy to live there after Dad.) I have been removed from everything I had ever known. My Dad had died, and I was forced to hold my mother's hand while she wrestled with her own devils. Now my cat was dead, I was alone, and some crazed behemoth wanted to kill me for trying to do him a favor. This was far from my land of blossoms…

I heard Mom come up the stairs at some point, and she begged me to let her in, but I refused to acknowledge her. I said nothing, though she had plenty to say. She cried and apologized for Mr. Peanut. She begged me to forgive her and she promised me she would get some help.

It was the same story I had heard a thousand times, the same promises she always made that she never followed through on. She talked a good game when she messed up, but she was soon back to her old ways of trying to find the perfect "balance" of pills that kept her at just the right level of numb. This never-ending quest of hers had become both of our realities.

One day she would be bedridden and watching the same bad eighties romantic comedies movies over and over again, and the next, she would be whirling around the kitchen trying to cook the perfect crepe. She rarely got the balance correct, and even when she did, it left her mostly incoherent.

I put on my earphones and tried to drown her out. She was gone when I got up to use the bathroom about an hour later, and I was able to sneak down and grab some cold pizza from the fridge. The cat and the pills were gone.

I went back to my room and locked the door again. I didn't want any of what she was peddling. I took out my laptop from under my bed and checked the Wi-Fi. It looked like she had finally managed to pay *that* bill, and I checked my phone to see if I had service. I did. At least she had done something right today.

I resumed my Viking research so that Mrs. Cliner and I would have something new to talk about in the morning. I didn't know what I was going to do about the angry lunchroom kid, but having to get to school early would be helpful on two fronts when you take him into consideration; he can't find me if I'm already in class.

As I drifted off to sleep, the bed felt cold in the absence of my cat. I thought of my grandma, my dad's mom, and her love of cats. There had always been cats around the farm. She would trade them treats for every mouse or rat they brought her. She told me that cats held secrets for a person, and that's why she had to have so many (always followed by a wink.) She told me this was the reason the ancient Egyptians revered the cat so much, even to the point of mummifying them and burying them with priests and priestesses. Mr. Peanut had been my pal and confidant. The only other being in this world I could talk to who didn't push their own agenda on me.

He still was a cat and did his own cat thing, but the nighttime was our time together. He would sit on my lap as I read, or play with things around my room when I was doing homework, and when we crawled into bed at night, he listened to me. He was the only thing in this world that listened to me, and now he was gone. I was completely alone again.

*

I woke up and dressed quickly. If I took a shower, I'd risk running into Mom and I still wasn't ready for that. I checked my phone, and I would have to hustle if I were going to get to Mrs. Cliner's class on time for my detention. I picked up my bag and made sure to grab a pencil. I paused in the kitchen, where I would normally feed the cat before leaving. His bowl was still sitting in the corner, and I grabbed it on the way by. I threw it in the trash can and then wheeled the can along the front walk, where it would be picked up.

I headed down the small hill where our house sat among its neighbors. My great-grandparents had been quite wealthy when they'd passed, and the house had been bequeathed to my grandparents, and then to us. I looked back at it, and noted how its run-down nature stood out amid its pristine and professionally manicured peers. I would really have to do something about that soon.

I made it to the bus stop, and I was the only person there. The bus came after a short wait, and as we wound through the streets, I noticed that we didn't have to make as many stops since it was still so early. It was only five-forty-five, and I breathed a bit easier as it looked like I would be on time for detention. One could never trust the bus.

It began to rain during the ride. I could hear the rumblings of thunder even over my music, and I watched as small drops began to appear on the window next to me. I remembered rainy days on the farm, back before Dad joined the Army. He couldn't do much workwise, so when he wasn't fixing something in the workshop, he would stay in the house with Mom and me. We would build a fire in the fireplace and put on silly plays. We would sing songs, and make s'mores for lunch, and then all three of us would end up falling asleep in a big pile of blankets on the living room floor.

I could feel tears welling up, further blurring the window scene, but I fought them off. Other kids got to be loved. Other kids got to be happy. I felt robbed. I felt cheated out of my family by my dad, by the Army, by my mom, and by life.

I was remembering what I had lost when I got off the bus. What I hadn't remembered was my busted shoe. As I stepped down onto the sidewalk, there was a puddle. Not a large one, but just big enough to give the gaping hole in my shoe a good drink.

I yelled out in frustration, but there was nothing I could do. Every day was becoming another nightmare, each with its own set of problems. My foot was totally soaked, I could feel it getting colder as I squished my way down the block.

I walked up the school steps and shook the rain off myself as best I could. I entered the dark hallway, quiet and free of students at this early hour. A janitor was there and he looked at me curiously as I came in, before he resumed his mopping.

As I approached my locker, I noticed that someone had scratched out the extra E in "deed," and replaced it with an A. I guess somebody had told Red his spelling was off.

I took out my History book. I figured I would probably need it right after detention for Mrs. Cliner's actual class, but I wasn't sure how this side assignment was going to work.

I squished down the hallway towards her room. She was giving me a chance. It was an opportunity and a break, the likes of which I hadn't gotten in some time. I didn't want to let her down.

I tried the knob of her classroom. It wouldn't turn. I noticed a piece of paper stuck to the door that read: "Morning detention has been cancelled today. Mrs. Cliner is out sick, and there will be a substitute for her classes. All detention attendees may sign this notice before six-thirty a.m. for full participation for the day."

I took my pencil out of my pocket and signed my name. Then, after looking at the time, added "6:20am" after my name, so that she would know I was serious about my new project.

Damn... After Mr. Peanut, I had been excited to have some one-on-one time with a sane adult. I'd also been happy to have some time set aside for us to talk about this cool new Viking stuff. My spirits dipped even lower... I didn't think that was possible. I wandered through the halls and stopped at the bathroom.

I went in, walked to the sink, and turned on the hot water. I stood on one leg and removed my faulty shoe. Then I took off my sock and stepped on the empty shoe. I didn't want my bare foot to be touching the bathroom floor, especially at a high school. Kids are gross.

I wrung out my sock, then ran it under warm water. I figured that even though it would still be wet, at least it would be warm for a little bit when I put it back on. I heard the door open and footsteps behind me. I looked up at the mirror and was surprised to see the pencil boy from the day before walk in. He was surprised too, probably at seeing someone else here so early, but then he got a funny look on his face as he saw what I was doing. "I got a hole in my shoe," I explained, and he smiled a little before turning around and heading out of the bathroom. I shook my head; he must be a bit shy with his toilet use, I concluded.

I stuck my leaky shoe on the end of the hand dryer. I turned it on and counted how long it took to turn off. Thirty seconds… this was going to take forever. I had probably pushed the button twenty times by the time I heard the door open again.

The kid walked back in, smiling again. I had jumped up and was sitting on the sink next to the hand dryer, and as he came closer, I noticed just how short he really was. From my perch on the sink, the kid only came up to my lower ribs, probably just over four feet tall. He walked right up to me and reached into his shoulder bag.

"I don't know what size your feet are," he said, "but these should work. Socks are relatively universal." He pulled out a folded pair of very clean looking white socks.

"I always keep an extra pair in my locker, but I've never needed them," he went on. "Looks like I was really saving them for you!" He laughed at his own joke, a child's giggle, with a little hint of a snort at the end.

I took the socks and mumbled a thank-you. I didn't know what else to say. I really didn't want to talk to him, or anybody, but the gratitude of having a dry foot all day had won out.

"My name is Nathan," he said as he reached up and pushed the button on the dryer that had turned off again. "I skipped two whole grades last year. I'm really supposed to be a freshman." I nodded at him; he was only trying to be nice, but it bugged me.

"Look, kid, I do appreciate the socks," I said. "That was really cool of you. But I've already had a bad start to my morning, hell, my life, and I came in here to be by myself. Please leave me alone." I turned away from him as I pushed the button again.

He gave a final "OK… and you can keep the socks," as he turned to leave. He sounded sad and I listened to his footsteps fade away.

I didn't look up again until I heard the door swing shut. I hopped down as I pushed the button and bent to remove my good shoe. I took off my other sock and threw them both into the nearby trash. When the air shut off again, I checked my shoe for lingering dampness.

It seemed pretty dry now and it felt warm as I slipped it on over my new sock. My mood lifted instantly and I felt bad about how I had treated Nathan. I had taken my hurt and passed it to someone that was only trying to help me. This isn't who I wanted to be.

I raced out into the hallway to see if I could catch him, but he was nowhere to be seen. I could always pull him aside after Mrs. Cliner's class. I checked my phone and saw there was still an hour until class started.

I headed to the library. I hadn't been there yet, but it was the only place to stay out of the rain at this time of the day. I walked through the covered atrium that connected the library to the main building and saw that the rain had picked up. It was coming down in sheets, the rain pouring off either side of the roof above me. I tried not to think about my trip home.

The library was warm and inviting. It had that deep smell of paper that was so unique to its kind. It was smaller than most, but it was shaped like a hexagon, which gave it a cozy atmosphere.

I haven't been inside *any* library in a while. While I had used to love going with Mom, it had become just another thing ruined by her addiction.

The librarian looked up at me as I entered and gave me the mandatory finger to the lips to indicate I should be quiet. She then pointed to the left and I saw an empty coatrack.

I nodded and set down my History textbook, so that I could take off my drenched coat. I hadn't even noticed how wet it was. I guess the shoe had taken precedence. I hung up my coat and looked around for a place to sit. There were some large beanbag chairs in a corner and I headed in that direction.

On the way, I passed a magazine rack that was filled with all sorts of donated subscriptions. I filed through them: *Popular Mechanics*, *Seventeen*, *Time*, *Rolling Stone*, and *CosmoGirl*, until I finally spied a *National Geographic*. The cover had the normal rolling landscape of some far-off land, but in the list of secondary articles I noticed a mention of "Norse Trade Routes." Perfect.

I went to the corner and plopped down in the beanbag. It gave a terrific whoosh as I landed and I wiggled around a little to find the best spot. The article was a few years old, so the recent discoveries weren't accounted for, but it provided a map of archaeological sites all along the lands of the northern Atlantic, all proven to be of ancient Viking origin.

I could definitely see a trail that led to North America, and was surprised that it had taken this long to find evidence of it. I finished the article and got up to put the magazine back. I was going to look for another, but I glanced at the clock on the wall and knew that I should head to class. Even with Mrs. Cliner gone, I should be responsible enough to get to class on time. Only I could control what I did. I thanked the librarian and went to put on my coat. It hadn't dried much, and it didn't look very comfortable, so I slung it over my shoulder and headed to class.

The detention note was gone. I assume someone had collected it at six-thirty, but the door was still locked. There were a few other early students hanging around outside, and I saw Nathan sitting on the ground reading. *Excellent*, I thought, *I can go thank him for the socks real fast before the substitute gets here.*

I started walking over to him. He didn't notice me as he was deeply immersed in his book. I got closer and smiled as I prepared to slump down the wall next to him.

Right before I did, a loud call echoed through the hallway. "HEY!" Nathan looked up from his book and jumped when he saw me so close.

"HEY! YOU!"

A sick feeling came over me as I realized who it was. I turned slowly to see for myself. There was Big Red standing with two other guys, all looking directly at me.

I did the normal "Me?" motion, and looked over each shoulder to check if he was referring to someone else. It was all theater. Everyone knew he was there for me.

"Yes, you!" said one of his cronies and he pounded his fist into his other palm. "You're dead meat, asshole!" Red began to roar and all three came rushing down the hallway.

I had never really thought about the term "saved by the bell" before, but just then I got a very literal example of its importance. Just as they started towards me, the bell rang, signaling the start of class. This also prompted the substitute, who had been in the room all along preparing for her day, to open the door for those of us who were waiting. The open door blocked the ruffians, and I dashed into the classroom. I sat down in a desk in the back row and saw all three of them poke their heads around the doorframe.

It was funny, just like a *Three Stooges* episode, each one appearing at different heights to see where I had gone. Their eyes found me as I laughed, which only made them angrier. "After class," Red mouthed, before the sub asked them if they were supposed to be in the room. They offered an excuse and she ushered them out of the way, closing the door behind them. Even then, I could see Red leering at me through the little window. I propped up my textbook and hid behind it.

He was gone when I looked again, and the tardy bell sounded as I lowered my book. I noticed that Nathan had taken a seat in the front row, as far away from me as possible. I wouldn't even be able to whisper an apology to him or pass a note. Damn.

The substitute picked up where Mrs. Cliner had left off. She began her lecture with the days leading up to the end of the war. Again, I knew this stuff, so I started planning my escape from Big Red.

I didn't know what class he was in, so I didn't know how long it would take him to get to me. Even if he left right when the bell rang, I figured I would have at least a thirty-second head start. There was only one door in or out of the room, so I would have to be fast.

I glanced at Nathan. He was fanning himself with one hand as the teacher droned on while furiously taking notes with the other. He then stopped, raised his arm, and asked if it would be OK to open a window.

I looked at the big row of windows along the side of the room and noticed they were all fogged up. The sub nodded permission and Nathan got up to let in some air.

This school was pretty outdated, and the windows looked like they were fifty years old, if not older. Each windowpane was about three feet long and two feet high, and along the bottom row were large latches in the middle. I watched as Nathan reached up and undid the latch and then pulled the top of the window down towards him. The window was hinged in the middle, and the bottom swung outward to reveal a foot-wide gap in either direction. Suddenly, I had an idea.

I raised my hand and asked if I too could open a window. The sub nodded, and I switched seats to sit by the back window. I twisted the latch, pulled the pane open, and looked out through the bottom. I was sure I could squeeze through the space. I leaned over and looked out to see what kind of drop there was, and I was glad to see that the fall wasn't big.

The rain was letting up, but there were huge puddles everywhere. I didn't care so much as I had bigger things on the line than a wet foot. My plan was that as soon as the bell rang, I would push my jacket through the open window, leaving my textbook behind to be retrieved later, and I would climb through. The sub didn't really know who I was, and I figured that even if I got in trouble, I would have a very good excuse.

I would jump out of the window and run along the back of the school until I got to the part of the fence I had climbed the day before. I would ditch the rest of my classes, and then, I don't know, change schools or something. This was getting ridiculous.

I wished I could just sit down with Red and explain how this had gotten out of hand, but now he only seemed to want revenge. I had only been trying to help him. But some people are more action than words, even if that action is violence. I stared out the window while the teacher went about her work until I could feel the energy in the room change.

Kids were no longer attempting to prevent their boredom; they were anticipating their exit. Papers were shuffled, bags were opening and being stuffed with books, and pencils were being stowed away. I looked up at the clock and I watched the minute hand slowly start to twitch. It skipped over to nine-thirty, and the bell sounded. It was on.

The other kids leapt up and shielded me from the substitute's eyes. I grabbed my coat and tossed it the six or so feet down into some bushes. I climbed up on the short bookshelf under the window and stuck my legs through. I turned over and lay on my stomach as I slid out further, and I gave one final look towards the front of the room.

The sub seemed oblivious to my actions, but Nathan was watching me. He seemed like he understood what I was doing but he still looked a bit shocked. I gave him one last nod before I dropped to the ground below.

I landed easily and grabbed my coat. The rain had stopped and I looked around to see if I had been spotted. There was no one there, so I put my coat on and started running for the fence. I had one more corner to round, and the climb, but I was feeling home free. I kept up my pace and took the turn going almost full speed. I didn't expect anyone to be on the other side of the blind corner, but there he was, the smaller goon who had told me I was to be dead meat.

We collided and were thrown back. He realized who he'd just run into and called out, "Over here!" as he scrambled to his feet. I was already up and headed to the fence before he was done yelling, but a quick glance around showed the other two running my way from both directions. I ran to the fence and jumped, grabbing as high as I could. I held on, but only barely. The rain had left the metal bars slick, and I only just kept from falling. My broken shoe was useless for climbing, as it provided no purchase with the tear in the rubber.

I kept going. I tried to reach higher and higher, attempting to escape, but I soon felt a heavy grip on my leg. I was yanked down and the two smaller boys pinned my arms back. I struggled against them, but I had lost a lot of muscle since the farm days, and they held me fast.

I was still fighting when I felt the first blow land. Right in the stomach, and with enough force to leave me completely breathless and sick. I doubled over, and the boys jerked me back up. The next punch landed right below my eye and I saw stars. It was a free-for-all after that. They let go of my arms and I fell in a heap. They kicked and punched me for what seemed like forever. I was lost in a fog of pain.

The punching subsided after I heard a small voice yelling at the boys to stop. It was getting louder, and then there was water, and I realized that the others had abandoned their assault to run. I raised my pounding head, and saw Nathan standing there with a defiant look, holding a hose attached to the nearby spigot. He snorted like a bull that had taken out the matador, and he turned to shut off the water.

My eye was swollen and bleeding. I was dizzy. I ached all over, and I felt completely humiliated having been saved by little Nathan. I tried to get up, but my head was still spinning and I crumpled back into a pile on the ground.

Nathan grabbed me under the arm. He pulled at me and heaved, trying to help me get to my feet, but I jerked my arm away. In the darkness of my eye, through flashes of pain, I saw the bloodstained blossoms that had carried away my dad. I got angry again; I would not be weak like him.

I tried to build a callus around my pain with indignation. I would show everyone just how strong I was; I didn't need anybody's help. I said so to Nathan as he took my arm again, but he was insistent.

"I said NO!" I yelled, and launched myself upward, sharply pushing Nathan back off me.

All of my pain, all of my suffering, all of my sadness went into that push. Even with only one good eye, I could see the complete betrayal and fear pass over his face as his small body flew through the air. I watched in horror at what I had done.

He was lifted up by the shove, and his body slammed into the brick wall of the school, a good two feet off the ground. His head smacked with a sickening thud, and I heard something snap as he crumpled to the cement. Nathan lay there, unmoving.

I panicked. I ran over to Nathan and checked to see if he was still breathing. He was, but it was slow and it seemed forced. I didn't know what to do. I didn't want to call an ambulance with *my* phone, but someone needed to. I made up my mind and ran for the office. I burst through the door.

"Something happened to Nathan!" I yelled at the secretary. "He needs an ambulance by the big fence on the south side!" He looked at me scared, most likely because my eye was starting to look like something out of a slasher film, but he immediately picked up the phone and dialed 911. I heard him starting to report the incident, and he called after me as I rushed out of the office, but I wasn't going to stick around. I hit the front door and it slammed against the wall as I rammed through it. It reminded me of what I had just done and I felt sicker. I kept running. I needed to get away from there, away from what was going to happen. I ran until I couldn't breathe anymore, and I was completely lost.

When I finally stopped, I found myself in a little community park, alone. There was a small swing set with puddles beneath it. A structure with all sorts of multicolored climbing implements led up to a platform that held a long tube-slide, also with a puddle underneath. I didn't see a good place to sit down until I walked further and noticed a toolshed under the shade of an old walnut tree. It had a good-sized overhang, where someone had set a crumbling bench along the wall, and it looked fairly dry. The seat groaned as I sat down, and it shifted a little to the side, but it seemed like it was going to hold me. I turned sideways and pulled my legs up to my chest. It was there, on that crooked old bench, with my head leaned against the shed wall, that I finally let it all out.

My dad and his selfishness, my mom and hers, Mr. Peanut, the farm, blood, all of those were forced on me, but Nathan... I had chosen to lash out, and now I'd hurt him... badly. It was too much. Holding in my own hurt was one thing, but unleashing that on someone else was something else. I shook the old bench with the great blubbering sobs of ten grief-stricken years.

*

The boy had fallen asleep on the bench after he ran out of steam.

He had had quite the tumultuous life up until now, and I could feel Jacob's deep-seated pain as our energy merged into one.

*

I was instantly awakened by a booming flash of consciousness.

It ripped us from the deep sleep Jacob had put himself into.

His body was thrown onto its back, and with a great groan, the bench sagged further to the side, but it held.

Though, it no longer mattered. My being intertwined with Jacob's.

The boy was overwhelmed with knowledge. His mind was thrust into both chaos and order at the same time. Thoughts and experiences took shape as he was given the knowledge of the very inner workings of life itself. In front of his eyes, he could see the constant flow of energy that danced and passed through all that surrounded him. He could even see small bits wafting from the eave of the building that hung above him. Everything was so alive, and in constant communion with everything else. He raised his hand in front of his face and watched as the waves of energy radiated from it. They mingled with all that surrounded him. It... balanced.

Jacob and the omnipotent embodiment of ever-loving light and peace became one.

I knew I was different now, but I was still the same. I was still me, but I was everything else as well. I saw my dad, but with the understanding of his choices and actions. I knew exactly what Dad had gone through during the war, and what he had witnessed. I knew that the horrible creation of "bad" energy that comes from those kinds of experiences does not remain on the battlefield. That it takes hold of a person and replaces bits of them, that they carry those bits with them for the rest of their lives.

Each negative life experience leads to more and more replacement, each replacement addressed by its host with a pearl-coating that is applied over time to protect the bearer from its persistent chafing. Every soul-crushing defeat, every attack on the spirit, every bodily assault leaves gaping wounds in our very being. A huge vortex of darkness swirls around the entire *whole*, a disrupting vortex that grows in momentum through the constant exchange of dark energy passed from one individual to another.

Dad went to war and he brought a pestilence back home with him. With it, he infected me, he infected Mom, and he infected the farm. Dad didn't know what to do with it, and nobody had ever taught him how to deal with coming home *from* war. So, he made it his own, and then transferred his virus to everything and everyone around him. Mom had taken her share of the energy, and used it against herself. It obliterated her inside…

An oyster makes a pearl when an irritant enters its shell. Over time, layer after layer, the grain of sand or chunk of rock is coated and hardened against the irritation. The obstruction is still there, but less of a nuisance. Mom's particular pearl-coating came in the form of a medicine bottle. And where she looked to outside influences to deal with her pain, I had taken my inheritance from Dad and stowed it deep within, like the oyster. I knew this energy was eating me from the inside out, even with its meager coatings of protection. I knew what I needed to do.

As I realized what had to happen, I drew in the deepest breath this body had ever taken, and with a whoosh greater than a beanbag chair in a silent library, I let it all out. I knew that a single human was incapable of fighting this perpetual internal war, and that ending the war was the only chance for survival and happiness. Human struggles are a concise army that rage inside an individual in constant conflict. But outside, they are dispersed as single warriors into the natural balance, where the positive energies that sustain *the whole* easily overwhelm them.

I felt the vile congestion leave Jacob's body, and it was replaced with the greatest understanding of love and kindness that humans are capable of receiving. He was now fully connected to the Earth and all that it held. His energy understood our mission of epitomizing compassion and empathy, so that we may end the stranglehold of the darkening vortex. I was now whole in a terrestrial body, once again the complete defender of the Us.

All of that had taken seconds. One minute I was a scarred teenager, and then boom, I was everything in body and knowledge. I sat up and put my feet on the ground. I looked around, awed at the connection I felt. I could feel the trees growing. I could feel the soil creating life. The very air was alive with the comingling energy of old endings and new beginnings. I stood and emanated my presence with a surge of light. "I am here once again; let's do this!" I called out.

My announcement was met with the human need for food. Tacos, in fact. Though there wasn't a good taco place within walking distance, there *was* the burger place by Mom's house. My stomach rumbled at the thought. I checked my phone; school would be getting out soon, so I could head home. I took a step, and felt the cold squish of my shoe and I suddenly remembered Nathan. I saw the balance now, and knew that I had only responded to him in a human way, but I still needed to know if he was alright.

I called the school and attempted to sound as old as possible when the school secretary answered the phone. "Hi, this is Mr. Johnson," I said, making up a last name. "My son just told me that someone was hurt at school today, and he wants me to see how the injured child is doing. Is the boy OK?"

"Hi, Mr. Johnson," the secretary said. "I am unable to divulge any of the boy's information, but nobody was gravely injured. I *can* say that it appears that the whole thing was an isolated incident, so there is no need to worry about your own son's safety."

"OK, thank you very much," I said and ended the call hastily before she could ask any questions.

Good. We hadn't hurt Nathan too badly, but *I* still needed to talk to him and apologize, and to share with him what I knew. There was no point in going to the school now that I knew he wouldn't be back until the next day. I would only be seen as the person I had been, not what I am now, and our message would be tainted. I would first focus on someone who needed it much more than Nathan, someone much closer to this human, his mom.

Well, I would *first* focus on burgers, then Mom. A look at a map-app told us that the closest bus stop was a few blocks away from the park. The wetness no longer affected our foot as we left there, but a crunching sound behind me made me turn. The bench we had been sitting on had completely collapsed. Puffs of dirt and debris flew into the air, and I called their essence to me. I took in the energy of its last dying breath and I thanked it for its service. It's off to be other things now.

I could feel the bus coming before it got to the stop. A kind of forward momentum wave from the speed and concentration of the people onboard. It stopped in front of me with a hiss of air brakes, and the door opened to let a few passengers off.

I took a seat in the front, one of the sideways ones, where I could see up and down the entire length of the bus. People were minding their business, reading books, listening to music, or looking out the window.

A baby began to cry and I watched as illuminating ripples of love were expelled from the mother as she lulled her daughter into a state of comfort. The energy was all around and bonded with all of us who were close by. A standing man smiled as the energy made him think of his own mother's love. A little girl patted her doll empathetically. I thought of the mom I was off to save.

But I also watched as this energy was suddenly dimmed by the angry voice of another. From a few rows back, a man was arguing into his phone, and he began to curse and scream at the person on the other end. From him, dark spikes of despondency jutted out. They overtook the positive influence the mother and daughter had shared.

The darkness filled the gaps around the others. The little girl, now clutching her doll, looked scared. The standing man frowned, reminded of how he had recently yelled at his own children. The bus stopped and the screamer got off, but his darkness remained. It stayed with everyone else, and when they got off, they would spread it to whomever they encountered. I looked on with sadness.

The bus dropped me directly on the doorstep of the burger joint. The air was heavy with grease and spiced meat. We only had about ten dollars on us, just enough for a medium-sized burger, fries, and a large soda.

I took our number and sat down. I watched as grumpy customers pushed their energy towards the workers, who fought back with kindness. I watched joy as a boy opened the prize from inside his kiddie meal. I watched heartache outside as people passed by a homeless woman, her energy almost nonexistent. I watched this change as a man dropped a five-dollar bill into her cup, and she thanked him as she ran inside to buy some food. I watched the balance sway back and forth.

My number was called, and I took my bag of food back out to the bus stop. I had five minutes until the next bus arrived to eat my meal and I devoured it. I must have looked a mess with my eye and my clothes askew and dirty from the fight and transformation as I took huge bites of the delicious burger with the delight of a child eating an ice cream cone.

As the bus pulled up, I realized my burger bliss had clouded my thinking, and I was standing at the stop for no reason. The house was only a few blocks away. My belly now full, I turned and headed up the hill to find Mom, and to finally ease her of her troubles.

The front door creaked as I opened it. The rain had swollen the wood a little. Nobody called out to us. The TV wasn't on, and the home was cold and still. We turned up the thermostat and went upstairs to change. Even though the wetness didn't bother us, it was not generally good for the human body, even when acting as a host to an immortal.

A pause at Mom's room told us that she hadn't been home since the day before. Her clothes still lay scattered all over the floor and the same red shirt lay in her doorway. It would have pained Jacob yesterday to think that she hadn't cared enough to come home, but we knew that the misery of her failures had probably kept her away. Killing your child's beloved pet was a big one…

I peeled off our pants. The one wet sock had been touching our jeans, so winding trails of water crept up the pant leg. I quickly donned sweatpants and a sweater as I felt the body start to shiver from the extra exposure. I put on new socks and went down to the kitchen, starting to warm up as we ascended the stairs. No sign of Mom there either. The kitchen was spotless after Mr. Peanut, and I wondered what she had done with him.

The kitchen had a door that led out to the backyard. The center of the door was a window still hung with great-grandma's hand-stitched lace curtains, and in between these, we could see something different outside.

There was a raised bed made of red brick on the edge of the patio. It had once held grandma's prized rose bushes, but those were long gone. Now, a fresh mound of dirt stuck up above the weathered edge. I recognized the energy coming from the earth.

I placed our hand on it. The mound was patted down and compact, and there was a tiny cross made out of popsicle sticks stuck into it. "Mr. Peanut" had been added in scribbled Sharpie. Part of Jacob had been scared that Mom would've just thrown the cat in the trash, so it was good to see that addiction had not completely drained her of decency.

I headed back into the house. It hadn't been that long since the burger and fries, but we were hungry again. The kitchen didn't hold much. Jacob would usually resort to school lunches and fast food to keep him going, but we needed more. I found cans of beans and powdered milk in the pantry, but those wouldn't do. I found a rotting potato in the vegetable crisper and threw it away.

The freezer was caked in frost, and held nothing edible, but there were two voids in the shape of fudge-pops that told us where Mom had gotten the sticks to make the cross for the grave. Gross, we hoped that she hadn't eaten them, they had been in there for a year. It wasn't until I moved the bag of sugar on the counter that I found something that would work. There, in all of their blue and orange glory, sat two boxes of family-sized mac and cheese.

It hadn't been around for long, but the easy-to-make dish was quickly becoming a favorite, maybe fifth in line behind tacos for Us. I grabbed the powdered milk – it would have to do – and we whisked it together with warm water in a large glass measuring cup. I grabbed the big pot that still sat on the counter from a week ago when Mom had tried making her spaghetti, but had burned the sauce. Jacob had spent an hour scrubbing the charred tomato charcoal from the pot afterwards.

I filled the pot with water and set it to boil. I mixed the cheese powder in with the milk and waited. Soon, grinning like a Cheshire cat, we were folding noodles and cheese together into gooey goodness. It got eaten right out of the pot with the large mixing spoon while we sat on the back porch with Mr. Peanut.

I couldn't count on seeing Mom before tomorrow. Her anger at herself would most likely be dealt with through a binge, and all I could hope for was that she lived through it until she could be helped.

Nathan was another story. I could see him tomorrow if we could manage to avoid the consequences of the school long enough to catch him. Even if Nathan hadn't told the teachers that it was Jacob who had hurt him, Jacob had ditched the remaining classes, and we would definitely hear about that.

I knew Nathan got to school before most of the students so we would have to make sure to catch him before the first bell. Maybe I could get to him right when he arrived.

I cleaned the pot and spoon and put them on a towel next to the sink to dry, then went upstairs and started the shower. The steam began to fill the bathroom as we undressed and climbed in. It was good to feel the cleansing water, and I washed away the bits of the day that held on to us.

Dirt and blood from the fight ran down the drain. Bits of leaves and sticks came out of our hair. All of it ran down the drain in a spiral of soapy water. Feeling physical things again was good, and I stayed under the hot water for some time.

It went cold eventually, and I was forced to shut the water off. I toweled dry and went to our room. I got new clothes fresh from the drawer and we dressed while we tried to figure out what next steps to take after dealing with Nathan and Mom.

Spreading the word would be hard at our age. I had certainly done it before, but it had been no easy feat. Adults don't tend to listen to children or teenagers, always believing they know better. Finding out how to spread our message, while wandering the individual's previous human transgressions, as well as doubt for someone claiming to be the equivalent of a new messiah, has been how we have spent eternity. Entering into a life that has already been established comes with a plethora of biases and prejudices against the individual human. Now Jacob will be labeled as a bad kid for his sullenness and aggression, and that will have to be remedied before we can go on and attempt to get our word out. This one will be different, but the same, as always.

I lay down in Jacob's bed and turned off the bedside lamp. The door had been left unlocked, just in case Mom came home, but she was usually gone for the evening if she wasn't back home by this time. In the darkness we could see the bright colors of energy ebbing and flowing throughout the room. They intertwined and swayed as the pull of one or another was stronger. We closed our eyes; tomorrow would be a big day. I let sleep take us.

*

The phone's alarm went off at five a.m. I awoke with new missions ahead of us, and new goals to accomplish that day. I dressed quickly and gathered what was needed for school. A double check ensured that we had the Viking research tucked into the backpack before we went and checked Mom's room. It was still empty. I dug through the pile of clean clothes that had accumulated on the floor and made a path to the closet. I pushed aside the plastic-wrapped clothes so that I could gain access to the boxes behind them.

Here, Mom kept what was left of Dad's things. I opened the first box to find a bunch of courting letters Dad had sent Mom when they were younger. The Jacob part smiled at the thought of the two of them so young and in love.

The next box held Dad's military uniform. It was clean and pressed and folded perfectly to fit into the box. I shuddered as I replaced the lid and moved it to the side. Underneath, I found what I was looking for.

It was a large box, with the flaps folded into each other to keep it closed. When opened, it revealed several pairs of Dad's old shoes. Work boots, dress shoes, cowboy boots, and old tennis shoes. It looked like a lifetime's worth of footwear.

I found the reward for our quest at the bottom of the box. We had to pull the top shoes out and set them aside, but deep underneath we saw a bright white pair. Years ago, Mom had bought Dad some running shoes. They were the really lightweight kind that barely felt like they were on your feet. Perfect for Dad to use to run up and down the dirt roads on the farm. But Dad wasn't having it. He questioned why he would want to do a full day's work, then go prancing around the property like a pony, even if it was to stay in shape. The farm kept him in shape. So, the shoes went into the closet and didn't come out again until after Dad died.

I took them and tried them on. Other than the contrast of the gleaming white against Jacob's drab clothes, they fit perfectly. I tugged the laces and tied them tightly, heaping the rest of the shoes back into the box and replacing everything the way it had been. I went downstairs and grabbed a waterproof coat off the coatrack just in case it was going to rain again. I even found an umbrella that was small enough to fit in the pocket, one of the cheap gas station types. I took a last look around the house and thought about turning the heat off, but it should be warm for Mom when she got home. I closed the door, locked it, and set off to find Nathan.

*

Jacob had certainly been right. There was a calm to the morning like at no other time of day, especially in the city. The energy that came with a city's midday rush was tangible. It was even visible in some places, like during that one life while we'd become "whole" while riding in a blimp that soared over New York City. We witnessed the city at one of its busiest times and watched the masses of energy flowing from it. Great crowds of humans expelling enough energy that the light rose shining, like a beacon. Good or bad, power like that could change Us forever, should enough people choose to focus it together.

The bus stop was empty again, but our ride soon came. The driver offered a "good mornin'," and we gave him a hearty "Gooood Morning!" right back. For once, the bus was empty and I sat down so that I could see the driver in his mirror.

"A bit early for school still," he said, glancing at me.

"I got in some trouble yesterday, so I have before-school detention."

"Ahh," he said. "I was a bit of a troublemaker myself when I was your age. Heck, I never really did settle down until around thirty-five or so. I sure hope my little girl doesn't have the same ants in her pants that her old man did. " He laughed and we joined him.

"Well, sir, you seem to have come out alright. Even if you did have a bit of an unruly start," I said. "She will turn out just fine with you as her father. Myself, I was blessed yesterday with the great hindsight and wisdom of all those that have come before us. I have obtained enlightenment. I am not the person today that I was yesterday, and I only hope to help build a better tomorrow."

He looked up at me in the big mirror and I could see his surprise, though he recovered nicely after only a short pause. "Enlightenment, eh? That's quite the accomplishment for a person your age," he said. "It took me a moment to realize that you were saying something prudent, as it would seem that most people of your age do not possess a level of such deep thought. Because of this, many times adults listen, but don't really hear. You have my full attention now, good sir, though I don't think I quite caught the last part correctly. Come again?"

"In short," we said, "I will only spread love and joy with my actions."

"Well, I think that that's as good a life goal as any! It's what all rational people *intend* to do. But, one has to be careful. For many people, somewhere in there, intention gets lost, and misunderstanding takes its place. Perception is an individual thing; be sure that you are constantly being perceived in the ways you want to be."

"Now whose turn is it to be wise?" I said, smiling. He smiled in return, then turned his focus to the early morning traffic.

I looked at him through *the whole*, reading his energy. He had been a relatively good man his entire life, and even more so after that settling down part he'd mentioned. He was a good father and husband, and he had worked this same job for almost fifty years. He was kind to animals and the elderly. He cut the rings on his weekly six-pack of beer for the sea turtles. He donated what he could to the local children's hospital, and he maintained his own positive balance. He was a good person.

I reminded him which stop we needed, and he wished us a good day as he opened the doors. Turning to him before going down the stairs, I held out our hand. We shook, and he grinned as I told him that he was a good person, and that the world needed more people like him.

"I do my part, but thank you," he said, and he was right. We *all* had a part to play.

There was a bench across the street from the school. It sat back from the road and had its own little cement pad that extended into the ivy lining the sidewalk. It was one of the donated city benches with a plaque on it. We read the sign as we sat down. "Donated by Ms. R. Fridae, 1987." No more information. Ms. Fridae may be a woman of few words, but her bench was comfortable and welcoming. From there, we had a clear view of the front of the building, and we could watch all of the comings and goings before the school bell rang.

The sky was cloudless as I watched it change from the darkened din of dawn to the light blue of a new morning. I watched the janitors arrive, followed by the eager teachers, as more and more cars began passing by. I watched the energy awaken, and coalesce around the institution of learning.

The first car stopped in the unloading zone, and a teenage girl hopped out of the passenger side. She slung her backpack over her shoulder and waved goodbye to the driver. She hurried against the cold up the steps of the school, and the big doors closed behind her. The car drove off once she was safely inside.

More and more cars began to show up and drop kids off. Slowly, we watched the teacher energy change. It was being matched by the energy of the students. Car after car came and went, none of them Nathan's. We waited. Groups of kids stood, despite the cold, all around the entrance. They gathered in threes and fours, sharing things that had happened the night before, or what was expected of them today. All attempting to find their own balance among the chaos of high school.

Nathan was nowhere to be seen. Arrivals began to dwindle, and the groups started to head inside. The first bell sounded and still no Nathan. The front of the school was completely empty, save for the occasional latecomer. When even those stopped, the final bell rang, and I wondered if I had somehow missed him. I contemplated sneaking around to the back of Mrs. Cliner's room to see if he was in there already. Just as I was getting ready to get up, a movement out of the corner of my eye caught our attention. There he was.

Nathan turned the corner and lost his balance, wobbling on his crutches. He didn't fall, but he had to readjust the metal poles under his arms. His foot was wrapped in a cast that rose about six inches above his ankle, and his head was wrapped in a bandage. He looked determined, and kept crutching his way up the small incline. But Nathan really didn't look like he should be at school today, let alone stumbling along by himself. I had to help.

His head was down as we approached him, focusing on every step. He was oblivious to ours. We could see his energy fighting with that which we had inflicted upon him. He had reached out, against his fears, and had helped a fellow student. The same student had rejected him. He still came to the aid of another, and was rewarded with anger and violence. We could see Nathan's spirit fighting the unnecessary battle we had forced upon him.

He didn't look up until we were standing right in front of him. His first clue that someone else was near was the brand-new shoes planted in his path. He looked up and started to instinctively offer an apology for the inconvenience. He trailed off into silence as he saw Jacob's body standing in front of him. As recognition set in, Nathan began stammering and backing away awkwardly on his crutches. His eyes grew fearful and he started jabbing a crutch in our direction.

"You stay away from me, you hear?" he yelled as he looked around for someone to help. He was shaking in his retreat. Jacob and I tried to call after him. We tried to get him to stop so we could tell him that we would never hurt him again, but he kept going. He limped into the crosswalk and started to cross the street.

He was halfway there when we felt it. The gusty push of energy that emanated from the high-speed movements of many people in close proximity to each other... the bus.

Nathan didn't see it. He was looking the wrong way and he turned back at us in fear. We acted.

The shoe company should be highly commended for their product. Hermes himself would have been proud to own a pair. Their weight barely resisted as our legs pumped to gain the necessary ground and our footfalls were cushioned in just the right places for a runner's stride.

Nathan had finally seen the bus coming directly at him. He panicked, dropped one of his crutches, and tried to hop to safety on his good leg. The bus bore down, its brakes and tires screeching as it tried to stop.

Our feet flew. We made it to Nathan just in time. The bus was only feet away when we were able to reach out just far enough to give Nathan one last good shove. We hoped he wouldn't be hurt much more than he already was, but at least he would be alive.

With Nathan now sprawling towards the sidewalk, we turned to face our own danger. In the split-second window, we recognized our bus driver friend from that morning. We saw his horrified look as he tried to steer the vehicle around us. There was no time to reassure him, or Nathan. Time only allowed us a knowing smile and wink at our driver friend, before his big machine slammed into Jacob's human form.

Our body was tossed up the hill towards the school and came to rest in the ivy along the sidewalk. We had fleeting visions of Jacob's memories as our corporeal essence gave its last spurts of energy.

The almond orchard of Jacob's childhood came to us.

The wind picked up, and the spring blossoms floated down all around us as we lay there.

They were healthy blossoms; well cared for.

Beautiful, unstained flowers covered us like snow.

*

Jacob and I returned. We dispersed throughout the infinite pool of Earthly energy, welcoming the unified solitude of Us. I had often died trying to save someone's life. My mission implored me to sacrifice myself, if I was given the opportunity. This didn't frustrate or hurt me, at least not compared to other ways in which I have died.

There is a freeness to it, a widening of consciousness that, as the single being with awareness of their recycled nature, only I am able to discern. My knowledge was my burden to carry alone, my personal data to analyze.

Humans cope in many ways with the pitfalls their lives bring, but most of them are not taught *how* to cope. At least not in helpful ways.

When children see people throwing fits over pennies at the grocery store, they believe this is acceptable. When children witness their parents give up on life, they are sent the message that life is not worth living. When kids get bullied, they internalize it, and then unleash the energy again in ways that they *can* control in attempts to regain their own power. They transfer the negativity that is thrust upon them to things that are weaker and more defenseless than they are. This is not necessarily learned. It is a natural response, but it is also honed within humans far more than elsewhere. Many must hurt others for their own meager survival. This is what it has become over time.

Not all humans, of course. There are still plenty of purely good people, but the numbers are dwindling, and imbeciles reign supreme. The issue is that those who operate in lifestyles outside the bounds of unity are enticing to those who normally would not be swayed. As the number of people working for unity decreases, the models for unity began to be lost. Greed takes unity's place, and the biggest atrocities that infect *the whole* can be traced back to this single selfish trait. Even with today's religions instructing people otherwise, humans have started to focus solely on their own interests. They have become their *only* priority.

It has not always been this way. This is not how it is supposed to be. Negative energy is freely passed around the world, and I can see its darkness flow with greater intensity than ever before. But, this is not our natural state, and all would have been lost long ago had it not been for the great pool of life essence that encapsulates *the whole's* entirety.

This past life as Jacob had been special in its way, but it wasn't the total electrification of grand scheme changes. It wasn't the same heightened sensations of those previous lives that had been supremely impactful. Something had certainly been started with Jacob's life, but it wasn't the buzzing tension of a world-changing life. It felt more like a small spark, but a small spark that had the potential to grow into the blaze of positive growth. The charge of excitement that I had felt before Jacob's life was still here all around the pool. It had not subsided like it normally does. If anything, it had grown. This was… different…

I then did something I rarely do. I looked back into *the whole*. It was easy to find Nathan's energy. It was very bright, and I could still feel his energy because it had been so recently entangled with my own. Even after watching someone die right in front of him, Nathan was bright. I watched him battling the new trauma, but he began to grow even brighter as he went on through high school, and then blinding as he went off to college. Good! He was moving past the ordeal, and hopefully using his experiences as a tool for good. He would never forget Jacob. Nathan would be just fine.

Jacob, I felt with me still. His ember remained, taking up residence within my eternal essence. This wasn't how it normally went down. Every other time my hosts would just dissipate and eventually start anew in *the whole*. This clutching was a change, and I needed to figure out why.

My thoughts were interrupted as I felt the nagging urge to be back among the humans. I don't know how long it had been, but my resting period really hadn't felt that long at all.

My hunger returned with full force. *The whole* was begging me to come again, and I was now being *pushed* into my next tour of duty. I grimaced at my stomach as I was expelled, and my last thought in our energy pool was "I better get damn close to a good taco place."

Tacos, mind you, are indeed a holy communion.

Chapter 2

I had to walk home alone. No one at school remembered that it was my birthday. Momma had only barely managed to recall, and had snuck in a quick "Happy Birthday" as she ran out the door to her car on her way to work.

I get a ride to school from Mrs. Johnson, our neighbor, and then Momma picks me up, but she forgot again today. I had only been back in school for a few weeks and she's forgotten a lot. Our house wasn't far, only about a mile. So, on the days Momma isn't thinking about me, I walk home, and do my *own* thinking about me.

I have my favorite shirt on today, but it got a little dirty at school when another kid splashed in a puddle by the garden. Hopefully, Momma can get the mud stains out. It's only my favorite because of its redness on it. I love red, and I love the big rainbow on the front, and I love it because my daddy gave it to me. This shirt, to me, meant my daddy.

Daddy is gone again during the week because of his work. He's a bus driver in the big city where I was born, but the city had gotten too expensive for us as a family, and we moved here when I was only two years old. I barely remember that.

Our home was about four hours away from Daddy's work, so he stayed in the city with some family during the week to save on gas and energy. But Daddy had to take some time off work earlier this year because he had gotten into an accident. I had overheard Momma and Daddy one night talking about it quietly as I crept out of bed to go to the bathroom.

Daddy had said that it wasn't his fault, but that someone had died in the crash, a boy. I peeked around the corner and saw Daddy sitting in a chair crying. His whole body was shaking, and he was making a horrible noise. I had never seen him cry before, and I didn't want to hear the noises that he was making, so I ran off and hid under my covers until I fell asleep.

After that, Daddy was home for a really long time. He only just went back to work last month. I miss him a lot, but he told me that this shirt would keep me safe when he was away.

I started towards our house, kicking a rock down the alley. I bet I won't even get a cake this year. I kicked the rock really hard, and it bounced off a garbage can with a dull thud before landing in someone's yard. Their dog started barking, so I ran past the house in case the dog tried to get out to eat me.

I grumbled, thinking about my problems, until the smell of water hit me. I decided then and there that I would treat myself to a birthday present: a stop at the creek. This small creek was fed by a lake to the west of the valley, and it snaked along the edge of the city. It held trout and bluegill. It was full of little crawdads and freshwater clams about the size of a quarter, both of which we would occasionally boil for a treat.

There were cattails and wild cherry trees, raspberry bushes that grabbed at you with their thorns when you got too close, and large oak trees from which people launched themselves into the water. Big rocks lined the water's edge, and these offered many places to sit and watch the green river slowly pass by.

Sure, I had been told never to go down to the creek by myself. But that was ages ago, when I was seven, and I'm eight now. Almost an adult, really.

The creek was just a few blocks out of my way. I crossed over the last street that bordered our town, and looked down on the creek bottom. I had been there before with my parents lots of times. We loved to sit and try to skip rocks, and I knew where a great spot was, so it was easy to pick my way through the giant boulders and tangles of trees and brush, until I was able to get to the water's edge.

It was quiet. The green flow eased lazily past and I saw dragonflies darting here and there, in and out of the cattails, searching for their lunch. I saw our good sitting rock not far away. It was a nice flat one, with plenty of good throwing pebbles all around it, and I pushed through the tall grass to get over there. I put my backpack down on the ground, took out my new Curious George library book, sat on the boulder, and chucked a few rocks to watch the water ripple.

It was always mesmerizing to me. The growing circles appearing out of nowhere, almost hinting at a hidden underwater world. I watched in silence as the ripples quieted, leaving my own pigtailed reflection. The breeze picked up, and the change in temperature gave the frogs their cue, and they began croaking their afternoon mating rituals.

As my last rock slipped below the surface, the plop of the water's response resounded through my head like the boom of a too-close firework. I was knocked back off my perch. I was completely stunned; I couldn't move. I lay on the ground looking up at the sky unsure if my eyes were open or closed, as before them passed human history in its entirety.

I witnessed the whole evolution of today's people, from the beginning until now. I saw humanity's greatest accomplishments and their greatest downfalls. I saw all of my past selves, all of my heartaches and failures, and all of my joys and successes. I saw humanity as a single entity, being drawn further and further towards negativity and the darkened points of no return. I saw technology, slowly at first, develop into machines that were meant to help, but that, in fact, pushed humanity further away from complete unity.

I watched almost all of the lessons I had taught as Jesus be bastardized, and then used for individuals to achieve wealth and prestige. I watched the very powerful prey upon the very weak. I watched entire harmonious societies founded on my teachings be wiped from our Earth by bigger societies that had praised conquest over peace. I saw the increasing influence of greed claim ever more victims as it took greater hold of *the whole*. I saw the darkness spreading, enabled by humans, and consuming all. I saw Us, and how became what we are.

Every inch of my body tingled with understanding, compassion, and love. Every muscle pulsated with the pain of the billions of time-strewn sufferers that have walked this planet, human, animal, and plant alike. Every bone vibrated in tandem with every other Earthly entity; the overarching frequency of us all. I took in *everything*, as I have learned that I must do in order to be ready. I had to encompass our entire being, *the whole*.

Birthdays were forgotten. Momma was forgiven for anything she had ever done. Human worry left us. In a fraction of a second, I had ended my time as that child of blissful ignorance, and yet again, we became burdensomely complete in self, knowledge, and purpose.

I had bumped my head on a branch when I fell backwards, and I sat up attempting to rub away the dull throb. It wasn't as bad as some pain I had felt in my lives, but it still stung. With my head down, and my fingers massaging my temples, I opened my eyes (I guess they *had* been closed) to see my favorite red shirt, now dirtier than ever.

The memory of a loving father's gift provided me the wherewithal to stand up. I rose, and soon found my balance. Curious George lay on the ground next to me and I bent to grab it. I hoped it wasn't ruined; it was a library book. I reached down to pick it up, but just as my fingers touched the book, I heard an unnatural noise. A branch broke as if stepped on. I straightened to look about.

I noticed that the creek bed had gone silent. The birds no longer sung; the frogs' croaks had faded to nothing. It was as if they all knew something and they hid. Now the creek was filled by excited laughter, and it grew louder. In a matter of seconds, I was no longer alone.

Being freshly "awakened" and bubbling over with jubilation and delight after my download, I got excited to have potential disciples so quickly. I could share my message with them and possibly enlist their help. They might be the first of many, and I needed to make a good impression. I took a deep breath and I prepared myself for my first task.

"Over here! I told you two idiots I saw one down here!" the first boy yelled as he rounded the bend and noticed me standing idly by the rock. He was older than me, probably thirteen or so. He was white, and was dressed in an American flag T-shirt and cutoff shorts. His friends followed close behind, four of them in total, and they all laughed when they saw me.

"Hey, you shor' did find one, didn' you?" one of them said as he took a long drink from the beer in his hand. He emptied the can, belched loudly, and threw the can into the creek next to me for the current to carry away.

It made me flinch; his blatant disregard for our collective being.

I watched the can float a little ways, and I turned back to the boys, ready to speak my message to them, even if this one might be a hard sell. I swiveled; arms held out by my side with my palms open to the boys. But just as I faced them, before I spoke, a rock struck me in the head. Inside, my brain exploded into a shower of colors, and nausea swept over me. With jagged waves of consciousness, I collapsed to the ground.

"Fuck yeah! You got that little piece of shit right in the forehead!"

"Did you see her crumple? Wow, what a shot! She went down like one of those faintin' goats that we saw on TV last month!" The group's hooting and hollering rang through the creek bottoms.

This wasn't right, not right at all. I needed to show them! I needed them to know! I rose quickly, still dazed, trying to regain my senses and my mission, but my inner human screams of flight took over.

I was pretty sure that I *could* outrun them, because I was the fastest girl in my class. I could make a break for it and come back for my pack later when the boys had gone.

I tried. I made a great dash for freedom, and I would have made it too... But the book... I had forgotten about the book.

My leg stretched out for purchase in front of me, but there was none to be had. My foot had come down directly onto *Curious George Goes to the Circus* at the exact moment the second rock slammed into the side of my head. These duel actions left me in a heap, vomiting into the creek grass.

I could feel them as they surrounded me, their footsteps and shouts growing louder. I could feel their hateful energy looming over me, wanting to tear every part of my little body to pieces, but I could not bring myself to get up. My body would not comply. My arms and legs were rubber, and I could feel blood pouring down my face.

As the punching and kicking started, I sobbed. I begged for them to stop. I called for my momma, and I called for Us to cease this senselessness. I screamed for *the whole* to help me.

My ears were filled with the boys' screams, bloodcurdling war cries of "We're gonna swing you from a tree!," "We should have kept you as slaves!," "Take that, you fuckin' darkie!," and "Fuckin' kill her!"

I mustered all of my remaining strength into one movement. With my last bit of energy, I was able to reach a single weakened arm up to American Flag in an attempt to stop the onslaught. I couldn't form any words, just a wailing moan of agony.

I aimed for his shirt as he bent down, so that I could pull him closer and ask him to stop. But he moved, and instead I grabbed at the only thing I could reach. It felt like a necklace. It broke apart. I could hear the distinct sound of a small chain hitting the rocks by my head as I clutched something in my closed fist.

I curled into a ball and tried to ride out the ignorance-fueled attack. I didn't know how much longer my eight-year-old body could last.

One kick either missed its mark, or was right on the money, because it connected solidly with my throat. The crunching sound of my own windpipe drowned out the boys' cheers for a moment, and I began gulping for air.

I could feel every heartbeat with pounding intensity. The hitting stopped when they saw the new struggle. My body started to flop and strain for life.

My bulging eyes, now fully open, caught sight of the flag boy coming closer. I gasped and gulped, yearning for breath, able to take in only a scrap of oxygen, further prolonging my agony.

The patriot inched closer and got down on his knees next to me. I locked eyes with him. His eyes were full of murder and disgust. It was a look I had seen many times. It was always the same, and it always gave me the greatest feelings of sadness I had ever experienced. A human, or any being, having strayed so far from our intended purpose.

Things were getting foggy and I felt our human-self losing the ability to think. Stars and Stripes leaned in close, right next to my ear. His breathed gusts of putrid beer and rotted teeth. He looked me right in the eyes, held the gaze, and quietly whispered, "The president says we don't have to tolerate y'all no more. Go back to Kenya, you fucking nigger."

He then spit on me, and gave one last kick that was strong enough to fling me onto my side. Their retreating footfalls echoed through the creek bottoms.

I felt myself dimming, the world growing increasingly fuzzy. My lungs were throbbing for air. My tiny body was quitting, giving out. I opened my eyes one final time, and, fighting the pain that encompassed me, I looked along my outstretched arm at my clasped hand. I caught a glimpse of what I had grabbed from the boy.

It was one of the greatest icons of sacrifice (even if it did not really quite happen that way). There, impaled directly in the middle of my palm, dripping blood, precisely at the point where fabled stigmata would occur, was a tiny golden crucifix.

I felt the last of me slipping away. As my body resigned, and my being prepared for its return to the energy pool, we offered our final gurgling gasp.

My vision was haloed by darkness and the last sight I had of this particular life was of my own crucifixion and grisly death, enshrined in a cheap fashion statement.

Our tears spilled and joined our blood.

*

The pain of their hatred stayed with me as I returned. This little girl was far too young to experience such horror, and yet this is what humans have let themselves become. I seethed, but the warmth of the energy pool was rejuvenating as it always was, and my ire began to ease. The pool was so refreshing after this particular ordeal that I did not even notice what had made its way back with me. The hypocrite's crucifix had pierced me much more deeply than I had thought possible.

What had seemed like a superficial wound was in fact powered by so much more. It had not only cut into the hand of the little girl, but it had cut a hole in Us as well. Fueled by hate and ignorance, the small gash had turned mightier than those boys ever could have expected.

I was no longer complete anymore, and I could feel the presence of the evil that had hitched a ride back with me. It was now here, in our pool... Fucking humans!

I don't know how to combat the evil in our place of creation; I have absolutely no clue. I *do* know that its presence here is an apex result of these idiots fostering and growing negativity within themselves. It has fed on them. Grown. Gnawed at my efforts of unity, and has spread to others like pestilence faster than I can combat it.

Hate, fear, greed, hubris. Humans have strayed far from the paths of compassion and love for all, instead choosing to love only their own, and reserving compassion for those closest to them. This is not the natural order of *the whole*. It is not the purpose of living, and it goes directly against my personal being and mission. When even the slightest diversion of natural order takes place, it creates a hole for the darkness to seep through.

It has taken all of this time, but the darkness is gaining an advantage. I have been fighting for many lifetimes, too many, but I have been unable to gain any ground in the fight against this sickness. It is here. The darkness has now begun to eat Us, and I could feel my anger rising again.

I searched for the energy of the little girl's father. It took me a little longer to find him than it took me to find Nathan. He wasn't so bright after the death of his only daughter. But I did find him eventually and I could see his brightness returning. Slowly at first, he began focusing his energy on civil rights activism. Brighter and brighter his energy grew, as he immersed himself further and further into the cause. Then I saw something peculiar. A long arm of energy began to emerge from the bus driver. It reached out, searching for something, getting brighter and brighter as his words were heard by more and more people. It was only then that I noticed another arm inching its way towards his. The two arms touched, and together they outshone all other energy around them. I traced the second arm back to its source, and was astounded to see that it led back to Nathan the Senator. The two joined in their missions. It made me happy. At least until my attention was yanked back to the encroaching darkness.

I could do nothing about this hemorrhoidal hate that now resides amid our purity. At least not right now, as I can feel the urgent call beginning again. I was already being pulled back into a physical form as I felt the pieces of myself rush in as they were yanked from their wanderings. The human hunger was sharper and more intense than the last time. I felt my energy being quickly forced together, and with a great BANG, I was expelled from the pool.

The interloping asshole would have to wait.

Chapter 3

The monastery is always cold, even in the summer. That's because it is old and built of large stone blocks that tend to hold the cooler temperatures. Between the everlasting chill and the humble rations that are meant to move us "closer to God," I am constantly shivering.

The priests told me that I arrived here in a basket, like Moses to the Pharaoh, but I didn't float. I was dropped on their doorstep by my mother, with my only possessions being a small silver cross on a chain, and a note saying that my dear mother wasn't able to care for me. The note listed my name and my birthday, so at least I knew who I was. I had been abandoned at six months old, and have known no other home than here.

Around the same time, another baby was dropped off. This was Billy. He is my best friend and we do everything together. We were the only ones who have lived our whole lives here, even the priests. We had each other, if no one else.

Sure, there were other orphans who came and went but it wasn't the same. They always seemed so much older, much more mature, and more well traveled than us. But the change of faces was nice, and we almost always had new kids to play with.

You had to grow up pretty fast around this place. There were strict rules and time schedules we had to adhere to. We attended classes, mostly about God and the Bible, but also some art, history, and math. I hated math. We had kitchen duties, bathroom duties, and other chores if we were caught doing something we weren't supposed to be doing. Plus, we had our private studies that took the place of normal "homework." This didn't leave much room for mischief (the devil's work, as Bishop McCants called it), but Billy and I always made sure that we found plenty of time to fit that in too.

Every once in a while, we would get a small bit of current gossip from Father Brian (the youngest of them), who would also play us the newest musical numbers on his iPod, but most of our outside info came from all of the "just passing through" boys.

They would tell us all about the newest movies and celebrities, or about all of the new "apps" and video games. About the big cities they had been to, or about vast farmlands they had grown up on. Our heads were constantly filled with things we didn't understand, and Billy and I reveled in every bit of it. Even when the rare occasion arose where we had been good all week and we got to go shopping at the market in town with the chef, we never got to experience anything but the chef's backside. So we loved hearing all about what the rest of the non-sheltered world did; it sounded like a crazy place.

Today is my tenth birthday. Father Brian had even given me a high five in the hallway as we passed each other this morning. Billy made me a card and snuck it under my pillow while I was asleep. In it was the only money he had in the world, five dollars, and the card said that it was for us to start saving so we could one day sneak out and go see a movie in the actual theater. A great idea and a great present, for sure! I hid the card in my bedside table underneath my Bible. I dressed quickly, feeling the birthday vibes, and I whistled as I headed to my first class.

My lesson was outside today as the weather was warm this time of year, even in the mornings, and Father Michaels liked to have our Latin lesson under the blue sky. I didn't mind, it gave me a chance to warm up for once. I found Father Michaels on a granite bench in the rose garden. The roses were in full bloom, and he shooed a bee away from his face. He looked skyward and watched the bright clouds that wandered in the blue sea above us. I sat down beside him and looked up.

"Equus," he said. This was Latin for horse, and sure enough, off in the distance, I saw a horse-shaped cloud running off into the horizon. It was now my turn.

I looked around until a shape appeared directly above us. "Lepus," I said as I pointed up to a rabbit-shaped cloud. Father Michaels nodded in approval. This went on for ten more minutes or so, until he sighed and said that we had to get some actual work done.

"We cannot sit and wait for the clouds to bring us all the answers," he said as he pulled out a worksheet for me to complete. He handed me the three-page packet. I moved to the neighboring bench and took out my pen. I lay down on my belly, as I liked the contrast of heat from the sun and cold from the granite of the bench. My constant companion, the silver cross, hung down from my neck on its chain and rested on my paper.

I went through the Latin worksheet fairly quickly; it took me about twenty minutes in total. "Father Michaels," I said, "I am all done with this assignment. May I go to the library to finish my math homework? As you know, it is due by the end of the day, and recently my chores have been…" – I paused as I looked for the right word to describe being assigned extra duties – "enhanced, by the other Fathers for some minor misunderstandings."

Father Michaels turned from his clouds to look at me, and there seemed to be a grin hiding beneath his gaze. "I am well aware of your *enhancements*. Are you under some impression that we Fathers do not communicate about the school's affairs?"

"Well, no," I managed, and I instinctively reached up to touch my cross in nervousness. Rubbing it always seemed to help my brain work better, and I quickly recovered. "But I also don't think that you all are of the same frame of mind when it comes to such things as discipline, and that some of you are much more lenient in your views of punishment. Please? I'm pretty sure that God wants me to know math…"

I almost lost it and giggled at the last part, and I saw Father Michaels's eyes wrinkle at the corners as he tried to hold back his own smirk. "Give me your assignment so that I may check it, first. Can't have you getting any more enhancements that might detract from other work, can we?" he said.

I nodded as I handed my paper over to him, confident that my work would speak for itself.

"Very good," Father Michaels told me after he had looked it over, "you may go straight to the library until this class is over."

I gathered my stuff and headed out as he turned back to the sky. However, Father Michaels did not become so instantly lost in the clouds that he forgot to warn me about making trouble along the way. "No shenanigans," he said as he looked my way one last time. The man knew me too well. But I agreed. I had enough confidence to add in a wink, but that was only because Billy wouldn't be out of his own class for another hour or so, and I never got into much trouble without him.

My walk to the library was short. Before I went in, I looked around to see if anybody could see me, and I dropped to the ground to roll on the grass. This was something for me alone, because Billy broke out in hives every time he did it. I stuck my arms above my head like a rocket ship and rolled. I loved the smell of the earth and grass, and the growing speed of tumbling down the small embankment in front of the library made me happy. Especially today.

I brushed myself off before going inside.

Father Daniels, or "the book troll," as we called him, was hunched over his desk, reading. He looked up when he heard me come in and scowled.

"Your hair is filled with grass," he said. "Do not be tracking in whatever manners of flora your hijinks have led you to be covered in into my library. Go out and shake yourself off, and I hope for your sake, you have permission to be here."

"Yes, Father," I said. "Father Michaels said that I could come and finish my math homework here. I completed my Latin assignment early." I walked over to a wastebasket and leaned over. I ran my hands through my hair swiftly to dislodge the grass, knocking plenty of grass onto the floor. I didn't think he could see the mess from where he sat, so I walked back by him and gave him a smile.

"There, grass free," I said and showed him my head. "I will just be over here quietly doing my work, no mischief, no trouble, no problems." I pointed and headed to one of the long wooden tables along the wall. I sat down and spread out my work, giving a little wave to the good Father before I settled in.

I honestly tried to do my math assignment. I pulled out the book, got my notepaper, and found a pencil that's tip hadn't broken off, but… I just couldn't bring myself to start. Mostly because I noticed a stack of magazine donations that had yet to be sorted. They were sitting by the window that provided me with light, and on the top of the pile was a magazine with a picture of a beach destination. The light blue water stretched out into the distance of the picture while a hammock had been strung up under the shade of a palm tree and a small table held two fruity drinks topped with pineapple slices. The white sands looked terribly inviting to me, and before I knew it, I was slinking behind a shelf to stay out of the troll's eyeshot. I grabbed the magazine and tucked it under my shirt as I made my way back to my table.

I moved my chair so that I would be facing the entrance, and my "work" would be facing away from the librarian, and I stuck the magazine into my textbook that I stood vertically on the table. I ducked down behind the book and started flipping through the glossy pages.

Sandals Jamacia was on the cover. They were selling package travel deals for only $999.98 that included airfare and accommodations. I wondered if I could borrow a collection plate for a few weeks. I wondered what the child labor laws were like in Jamacia. I could be a pool boy or something, though I didn't know if they even *had* pools so close to the ocean. A beach boy then.

I flipped through the pages, a bit faster now that I was losing interest with the realization that I most likely wouldn't be able to go to a beach like that anytime in the near future. I turned past all of the fancy hotel adverts and the exotic recipes, until I thought there wasn't much left. The pages were filled with smaller acknowledgements of photographers' credits and the names of those who did all the grunt work making the magazine possible. But the last two pages held something much different than the rest of the magazine. Here was a simple article, with no pictures, entitled "The Rise of Racism in the 21st Century."

Racism wasn't exactly something that we encountered here in the walls of the monastery. The clergy were all white. I was white, and Billy was white, but orphans of all different shades came through our doors, and they were all treated the same. *Equal suffering for all!* The article intrigued me, and I settled down to read it.

By the time I was done, I was wholeheartedly offended. Not as a white person, but as a human. *How could we still be treating people so horribly in a time when we are supposed to know better?* The article listed all of the ways in which the purported freedoms of this country had been denied to those who were not white. Not just that, it listed instances *from this year* of racially driven murders. One was a really little girl who had been beaten to death by other kids... KIDS! I felt sick. Where was God in all of *this*? Was this really the eternal suffering and sin that led to piteousness, because to me it just sounded like people were evil. Were our purported freedoms and equalities only illusions so that the wealthy could just continue on with their bigotry and greed, only now in the shadows?

I hadn't expected to feel so depressed on my birthday, and I gave up on reading or homework and rested my forehead on the cold table. Staring down at my shoes, my vision blurred between them and the much closer cross that dangled from my neck. It all seemed like a bit of a lie now.

"Happy Birthday!" shouted Billy into my ear as he poked his head through the stacks behind me.

I jumped, my cross leaping up and catching me just below my eye. I alternated between holding my ringing ear and testing the small cut below my eye for blood as I gathered my math book and the magazine back onto the table. I then replaced the chair.

Billy had been loud enough to earn a hearty "SHHHHHH" from Father Daniels, and the scolding replaced my deep thoughts as Billy and I laughed at his sternness. We tried to stifle our guffaws, but we could hardly control ourselves. I packed up my stuff as quickly as possible, tossed the beach magazine back onto the pile, and we hightailed it out of there before the book troll could catch us and send us to the kitchen for dish duty.

We made it to the large wooden doors, but that wasn't quite fast enough. We heard him yelling after us about running, but we had already made it out into the open. He was chasing us. We rounded the outside corner of the library, and we could hear him close behind. Just as he was about to reach us, we dove through the small opening in the hedges that served as the gateway to our little hideout.

There, in our safe spot, the bushes had made their own tent of sorts; Billy and I used it as a clubhouse. We had found some small rounds of wood we used as chairs, and the ground was littered with bits of toys that had been left by others or donated to the orphanage. There were a few small boxes that held our tattered comic books along with some other odds and ends, and a flat rock we had brought in for a table. This was our spot, our fortress of solitude.

We muffled our laughter with our elbows as we watched the hurried troll pass by our leafy shelter. When he was out of sight, we dove for our snack stash. This was sealed in an old coffee can I had stolen from the kitchen.

Billy has been on morning chores this week, so we hadn't had a chance to talk to each other yet, and with mouths full of pilfered communion wafers, we began chattering away to one another like chipmunks.

"Did you get to say goodbye to that boy Jon? He left today," Billy said right as I blurted out, "Father Brian gave me a high five, right behind Bishop McCants's back!"

"No, Jon was gone before I was done with prayers in the chapel this morning," I said. "He was a funny one, eh?"

"Ha! Father Brian is so awesome!" Billy exclaimed, and went on. "Jon said to tell you happy birthday, if he didn't see you, and he gave me something for you. Said we had to open it together." Billy reached into his back pocket bringing out a wrinkled handmade envelope with "have fun!" scrawled hastily across the front. I smiled as Billy handed it to me. What could it be? We'd had some good talks with Jon about life, school, and girls, but it had never been anything special. He was just another boy passing through.

"You go ahead and do the honors, it's your birthday," Billy said. I turned the package over and started to take off the tape. There was quite a bit. Whatever it was, Jon had wanted it sealed up well.

Billy reached back into the coffee can and retrieved the small kitchen knife we kept in there for any snacks that needed to be sliced. I was able to work the knife into the corner of the package and slice through the laminated layers. I looked up at Billy again, who had inched closer to better examine our treasure, and smiled. "Let's do it together," I said as our excitement grew, and offered him the open flap while I held the rest. He lifted it, and we saw what appeared to be a scrap of shiny magazine paper. Billy pulled it out.

It was folded and had been creased and handled many times, as it was quite worn, but it was still shiny. The part we could see was just words, some interview with a sports star, but then Billy started to unfold it. Our eyes widened as we realized what it was.

It was a picture. Not very big, and wouldn't have been worth anything to anyone other than us, but Jon had left us something special.

In the picture was a woman kneeling on the beach among large, pitted rocks, a big wave crashing directly behind her. A tasteful picture in general, if not for the woman's bare, sandy breasts glorified by the sun's rays.

We stared at each other dumbfounded. Billy and I had never seen someone so beautiful, or so naked, in all our lives. Even the pictures of the old Greek statues were nothing compared to this. I took it from him, my shaking making the paper jiggle, so it looked as though the woman's breasts were bouncing. We couldn't believe our great fortune.

Who knows how long we sat in our state of shock? It was probably only minutes, even though it felt like hours, but our trance was broken by the thundering call of "Boys, you *will* come out of those bushes, now!" We both jumped. It was Bishop McCants.

We each grabbed the picture to hide it and accidentally tore it in half. I shook my head from side to side, staying silent. Billy understood, and we both dropped the pieces of the page before we crawled out of our hiding place. If the Bishop was looking for us, we were going to be in very big trouble. He only had to deal with us when it came to the "grave transgressions."

As we crawled out, he abruptly seized us both by an ear and began booming, "Father Daniels has just reported that you two have been causing a ruckus in the library again. What are you two thinking? I have had it about up to here with you two! What have you been doing in the bushes?" He didn't wait for our answer, simply let go of our ears and crouched down, peering into our hideaway.

My half of the page had fluttered close to the entrance as we'd rushed out and Bishop McCants saw it. He picked it up and stood as he looked it over, peering at the page over his small glasses. His face grew red. "Pornography is a heinous sin." His voice was a whisper.

We really didn't know what to say, so we stood there hoping he would let us go with a warning. But, instead, he folded the page and stuffed it into his robe. He turned back to us, grabbing our ears again and said, "Library disruption *and* pornography! Add those to the dead rat we found hung up in the kitchen pantry, as well as the spitting in the holy water last week, and you both have committed grave transgressions."

He dragged us towards the kitchen, our ears on fire, as Billy and I desperately tried to keep up with his pace.

Billy was first to protest. "Sir, it wasn't his fault. I scared him in the library, he wasn't doin' nothin' but his math problems! Please don't blame him! And I am the one that put the rat in the pantry because Chef wouldn't give me a cookie, even after I helped out extra," Billy pleaded with the Bishop.

"Ahhhh!" we both screamed as the Bishop quickened his step and gave us an extra yank, but Billy persisted. "Please, don't punish him on his birthday! It was me!"

With that, the Bishop stopped dead in his tracks. He looked down at me and he seemed confused. "Tenth birthday," the Bishop muttered.

Billy saw the opening and jumped on it. "Yeah, how would God feel about you making a fella do extra chores on his birthday? I don't think he would be too fond of that!"

But his pleas fell upon deaf ears. Bishop McCants seemed to come to a serious decision with a nod, and began towing us along again while he murmured to himself.

Billy and I caught each other's eyes a few times across the Bishop's midriff, but the angry old man just kept on marching us and babbling about "God's wrath."

We arrived at the kitchen and the Bishop all but threw Billy through the doorway. Billy stumbled on the stone steps that led up from the garden door to the kitchen, but caught himself before he fell on his face.

"Twenty more demerits for Billy, Chef. Library disturbance and pornography, and he is also the one responsible for the rat." Father McCants slammed the door shut, but not before I caught a final glimpse of Billy, his face frozen in worry, the grinning chef looming behind him, intent on revenge.

This was *not* normal procedure. Every other time, Billy and I would ride out our punishments together. Both of us on dish duty for switching the cooking oil with the holy oil (holy omelets for all). Both of us raking leaves because we had jumped in the pile the gardener just finished raking. Both dusting books, cleaning toilets, polishing pews, not being spared "the rod."

I had a bad feeling about this change. We didn't head towards my room for confinement like we usually did when I was being punished. Nor did we head to the yard for raking duty, or even to the chicken coop for a cleaning. We walked past all of that, and the Bishop dragged me right up to the huge wooden doors of his own quarters.

I had been here a few times over the years. Once when the Bishop had a bad flu and Father Brian let me bring him some flowers from the garden. (He never even thanked me, but that was probably because I had brought him wild-mustard flowers and he was allergic.) Another time when there was an urgent letter from the Vatican, and I just happened to be walking by at that moment, and was sent to Bishop McCants's room to quickly deliver the piece of mail.

I did not like the place, not at all. The room was bare, even for a priest's room. There was a bed and a nightstand, a desk and a chair in the corner, a dresser, and a large wooden crucifix on the wall. A large stone Bible-stand sat by the bed, a single round carpet next to the desk, and there was a smaller wooden door towards the back that led to the closet.

The place had a very strange smell, like rotten oranges, and for some reason, I was sure this was where my never-ending cold was coming from.

My teeth chattered as the Bishop aimed me painfully by the ear into the corner by the dresser, and I slumped down the wall while clutching the side of my head. It felt like it was on fire.

I sat there, fairly terrified, as he crossed the room and approached the closet door. He was praying, muttering constantly to himself in Latin, and he moved like he was the only one here. He turned the handle and the smaller door opened with a long, drawn-out creak. He disappeared into the closet, searching for something, still going on about God's divine punishment. I heard thumps and bangs as he moved things around, searching for something. Finally, he brought a chair of sorts out of the dark closet.

At first glance it seemed like a normal chair, but it had a small shelf on the back, like an extra storage space for the person sitting behind you. In the backrest were two holes about three inches wide, and there were a few old and cracked leather straps attached to it in different places. The Bishop moved the chair further into the room and went back into the closet, only to reemerge holding a large wooden paddle that looked very smooth from use, and was possibly stained with blood. It too had the sign of the cross seemingly burned into it, and it had a leather strap that ensured that it wouldn't fly out of the person's hand during use. The Bishop placed the paddle on the dresser and then slid the chair into the middle of the room, now quietly praying to himself for guidance and a steady hand. He made the sign of the cross with his fingers over the chair, and he bent down to remove the ends of the leather straps from their buckles.

He turned to me. "By the power of God, through all of His wrath and through all of His glory, by everything that is righteous and chaste, I command you to kneel upon His throne."

Bishop McCants's voice grew deeper and more frightening with every word. My small, shivering presence was no match for this holy man. When I didn't move, he grabbed me by both ears, dragged me to a standing position, and flung me into the chair, forcing my knees into the seat as I landed.

He pulled the straps down over my calves and cinched them, and then grabbed my hands and stuck them through the holes in the backrest, tightening those in place as well. The leather straps burned against my arms and legs as I struggled to move, but I couldn't get any leverage, and the position of the chair forced my face to lie on the little shelf.

He then grabbed me by the hair and lifted my head. He looked me in the eyes, but said nothing as he slid his Bible onto the shelf beneath my cheek, my cross coming to rest on the top of the great book.

I gasped as he reached under me and unbuckled my pants, sliding them down to my knees. I was helpless. Completely confined, with my naked rear end exposed. The first blow came with the wrath of God, or at least the wrath of an oppressed Bishop, because I screamed bloody murder as the pain wracked my body.

He did not stop, nor did he seem to care about my screams. I pulled and writhed against my restraints, trying to escape the great onslaught of blows, but the chair was heavy, and it did its job well. Again, and again, the holy oak landed with stomach-churning thwacks.

I twisted my head trying to escape, trying to find some way out of this, but there was none. My sobs grew heavier until I was having trouble breathing. I began choking on my own gasps and phlegm and I threw up.

I watched through teary eyes as the vomit flew through the air, most of it landing on the floor, but a good bit began to seep into the leather bindings of Bishop McCants's Bible.

The beating finally let up, and the Bishop flung himself into the desk chair with great gulps of air. He looked at me and asked between deep heaves, "Have you witnessed the Lord's glory yet, my son?"

The last part stung, given my lack of parents and all. He was no father of mine, and he never would be. *Real* fathers would not treat their children this way. Before I knew what I was doing, I heard my impudent self saying, "No, not quite yet, your holiness. I have not yet seen the blueberries that I'd had with breakfast, and there's still a bit of this Bible for me to cover."

This was apparently not the right answer. He seethed. I could see him filling with rage, his eyes suddenly bloodshot, and I knew that I had quite possibly gone too far this time.

The Bishop began again with the Latin, as he shook uncontrollably. He got up quickly and started to pace in circles around the tiny carpet under his feet. I didn't understand what he was saying, most of his words were running together, but I was pretty sure that the devil had gotten ahold of him.

The chair contraption creaked with my own body's tremors as I grew more scared. The smell of rotten citrus, old leather, and bile singed my nose as the evil walked back around behind me.

"You have too much spirit, my child. Such spirit cannot effectively commune with God, as it does not include humility." His voice was eerily calm. "The church has ways of breaking such spirit. For years, we have driven the devil from your kind. You flaunt sin, you mock scripture, you take the lord's name in vain, and you never repent! You, *my son*, will receive *the* divine punishment."

It took me a moment to realize that the shrieks were coming from me. They sounded far off and faint, but the pain was what brought them home. I could feel my little body tearing as he entered me, and I could feel the warm gush of blood as it began pouring down my thighs.

Over and over, he thrust himself deep into my frail being, my insides straining and ripping from the force. I have never felt so much pain, nor such helplessness. I called out to God and told him that I was sorry. I pleaded for forgiveness. I wailed my repentance, but nobody listened. The agony grew to be too much, and I began to lose consciousness.

From behind me, I heard the guttural sounds of the Bishop reaching an apex. With a great pull on my body, he jabbed into me one last time. I could feel him unload his warmth inside of me and we both screamed out as a blinding flash took over my brain.

In a microsecond, my purpose had found me once again. I lived each of my lives over in the blink of an eye. I watched our world, Us, become what it is. My ever-presence took over the wounded child's body, banished the pain, and eased his terror. I was livid at what I had been awakened to. This type of thing had happened in other lives before, of course, but that never made it easier.

The stench of the room had become empowering. It was the smell of the true devil, my enemy, and it allowed me to easily snap the weakened straps that had confined the boy. The body's shivers were finally gone. *I* knew that the shivers were because they had been starving this boy his whole life... an orphan. Men of the cloth, starving orphans.

I rose, with much more spirit than this *Bishop* could possibly imagine. I left my pants around my ankles so that this man would have to face what he had done to an innocent child, and I turned towards the hideous beast who had collapsed in his own filth on the floor, a pathetic heap.

I knew from past encounters that such people need to be spoken to in their own language. If you don't speak their lingo, they don't hear what you have to say. He was a cowardly child, and I addressed him as such.

"*My* son," I boomed, using as much command as I could muster from the small body, "it is YOU who has committed the most grievous of sins, for your sins are done *in* the name of God, and against the innocent! It is *you* who needs to face the depths of hell for your depravity! It is *you* who will receive divine punishment, for I am the divine, BITCH! I am God's manifestation, His ultimate creation, His *true* son, and I find *you* to be a heretic, and Satan incarnate." My voice was no longer that of a child.

The Bishop looked up at me through eyes growing wide with terror. He saw the power and the truth behind my accusing glare, and he recognized every bit of the metamorphosis that had just taken place. He could feel my presence. He could feel *the whole* surging, pounding with me at its helm, and he knew what I said was true.

I went on, "You prey upon the weak, and you use the word of God to satisfy your unholy lusts. You are the epitome of hypocrisy!" With the last word, the windows in the room rattled, threatening to shatter. He shrank to the floor.

I couldn't help it, this time I went full metal Muhammad on his ass. "Dude, you even have a special chair for the occasion, you sick fuck! If there really was a hell, you would be first in line for the bleach enemas! You have taken MY great teachings of peace and compassion, and inserted your own delusion of righteousness. You are the worst kind of being, and I should fucking know."

He pleaded with me, begging for absolution. He crawled to me and grasped my leg, kissing my feet without any care for the blood, the shit, or the cum. He laid his head on my feet. His sobs were the only sound in the room, and I could feel his trembling tears. I couldn't exactly kill him, my purpose doesn't let me, but I could definitely make his life horrible until he *did* die. He was no longer a Bishop, no longer clergy at all. Just a sad, dirty, old pedophile who had been caught, and was begging for mercy.

I knew his life, as I had witnessed it many times. He was not fully to blame, as he himself had been abused as a child. He was taught that this was the way, that this was sometimes the only path to bring someone to God. But it was a path that should be "reluctantly strode," with the priest bearing the brunt of the burdened sin. What crazy logic. Ultimately, all they had to do was ask for forgiveness, right?

My being would not allow me to do it, though I could probably figure out how to smite him if I tried hard enough. I could forever rid the world of a supreme source of horror. But my compassion won out in the end, as it always does.

"Deep in the Andes is an old retreat of mine. A cave," I told him. "Here, you will spend the rest of your life in solitude, forging for whatever meager scraps you can find." I issued these commands, and waited for a moment before continuing. "It is a place of remembering, and you will do well there alone, without your religion, with only these evil memories to keep you company. You will die there. No one will remember your name, save for those you have abused."

He looked up at me with thousands of different emotions dancing behind his eyes. Anger, frustration, fear, sadness. It was like a bingo cage, spinning and rolling, until it stopped on one of the balls, and he slowly nodded. "If you so command it..." he said quietly.

He got up shakily, making sure to pull up his pants, and he dusted himself off. "You truly are righteous not to strike me down where I stand, and for giving me a life of penance," he said. "I repent my life of sin, and I hear your compassionate command."

He was fully standing now, sturdier than before; I didn't like that. He had always stood hunched a bit. He moved closer to me. With outstretched arms, he moved in for an embrace. I flinched at his approach, but knew that a finalizing act was necessary.

As much as it made my skin crawl, I let him hug me. I have hugged many a wretched soul, one more would not hurt me, but this man was truly repellant. He pulled me into his cassock while my arms remained at my sides. It was then that I learned that the smell was him. *He* was the deep stench of soul-rot, emanating from the very energy-consuming darkness that plagued and threatened our entire existence.

He began praying again as the pressure of his hug increased. His arms wrapped more firmly around my head, pushed my face into the stench, and I began to struggle for air. The black wool, which I had once admired, was pushing throat-clogging fibers into my mouth as my teeth attempted to gnash their way free.

Tighter and tighter he held me. My arms and legs kicked at him, but found no purchase in such close proximity. He was very strong, despite his frail appearance, strong enough to overpower a ten-year-old, and I was losing the fight.

I began spasming as his words rang through my ears. "Forgive me, Father, for I have sinned. Forgive me, Father, for I have sinned." Over and over again.

I was granted one final reprieve of breath as he pushed me from him, and I watched my necklace arc in flight as I fell to the floor. I gulped for air. I looked up into the eyes of my murderer, and saw the pure evil that lurked behind his holy indignation. He was no longer human. The darkness had fully taken this *man of the cloth*. It was everything inside him now. It called to me.

I was helpless, and the darkness engulfed me as the large stone Bible-stand was toppled onto my head.

*

I can still feel this fucking guy's stench eating away at my being, at everything that I was. It clung like a putrid shadow, and it followed me into the pool. More evil had been brought back with this life. It shot through the light and joined its kind, and *the whole* further dimmed. The eternal light was being slowly converted. The destruction was growing faster. Humanity was deep amid a vortex of de-evolution, and I could feel my influence slipping away from it all. All of my eternal work was being threatened. If I had a human body, I would be seething.

Even now I could feel little parts of me being corrupted, and with anger, I realized that it was not just taking me, but it was taking our collective knowledge as well. Little blips of memory and purpose were slowly being stripped away from the entirety of Us, being snuffed out into nothingness. I could see the darkness growing in our great place of creation. This would lead to the end, if it wasn't already.

I tried to look for the Bishop. I wanted to see him meet his fate, wanted to see if he would pay for my murder. But I wasn't strong enough. I even tried to check in on Billy, but I could no longer focus enough of my energy to look into *the whole*. I was losing this fight.

Not that there was any time for spying, analysis, or even rest for that matter as I felt a new life immediately pulling me to join it. The sudden feelings of starvation that hit me were gutting. Our energy was quickly shoved together, and we were sent off instantaneously.

Chapter 4

We had lost the game, and I knew Dad was mad. Everyone knew he was mad; we all knew his tells. He hadn't said anything to me on the way back to the car, but his temples always pulsed when he was angry, and they hadn't stopped pulsing since I had walked off the field.

Mommy had whispered "Great job!" when she gave me a hug before I ran to the locker room, but she definitely couldn't say anything in front of Dad. Even my big sister, who was sitting next to me in the backseat, was absently chewing on her hair, something she only did when she was really worried.

I didn't want to play football. I had never liked sports, except for some of the video games that Dad had, but even those were just OK, and he never even let me play them much. But Dad told me I needed to play football in order to toughen up.

"You'll never be a man if you don't learn how to take a hit, son," he'd said. "No, you can't join the chess club, I'm not gonna raise my son to be a pussy." And of course, "Put that fucking doll down, dolls are only for girls and fags."

These pearls of wisdom were usually followed by him storming out of the house and not returning until late at night when he was good and drunk. When he did come home, he would yell at Mommy for letting me become too soft; sometimes he would hit her.

He was able to sign me up for peewee football, even though I never asked him to. He just came home one day and told me I was playing. He said he'd "pulled some strings" in order to get me on the roster, which included me lying to the officials when they asked about my age. It was what Dad wanted though. So, against the wishes of the rest of the family, I was now a football player.

I was playing in only my second ever peewee football game while my older sister stood on the side with the rest of the cheerleaders. (Because that's where the girls' place is in sports, being the "weaker sex" and all. They had to support the men.)

Halfway home, Dad finally spoke in a low, controlled voice. "You could have cheered better… you were off from them other girls, out of sync," he said to my sister, looking at her in the rearview mirror.

"Yes, Daddy," she said. "I'll make sure I try harder next time. I'll work on my timing this week."

He turned his eyes to me in the mirror, squinting. "Son, that was a pretty pathetic performance out there on that field today. Even if this pansy liberal league don't keep score, I do, and your team lost. We. Do Not. Lose."

It was almost scarier when he spoke in that low tone. I would almost rather he yell so that I knew he was angry. Dad suddenly slammed his hands on the steering wheel and yelled, "I fucking took off from work for that shitty performance! There is no middle ground in life, SON, only losers and winners, and I'll be damned if you're gonna be a loser!"

His temples were now pulsing with rage. Mommy tried to calm him by reaching over to pat his arm, but he jerked it away and continued. Mommy drew herself up against the car door, attempting to make herself as small as possible.

"You didn't catch that very easy pass, the same very easy pass that we have worked on every fucking night for the past three weeks!" he yelled. "I will not have a loser for a son! Why can't you be more like those other boys? They have no problem catching the ball! Fifty sit-ups, fifty push-ups, and twenty laps as soon as we get home. And there better be some goddamn improvement at the next game, both of you!"

When he stopped, Mommy tried to point out that I would need to eat before I could do a bunch of exercise, but Dad was having none of it, and he shot her a look. "He can eat when he's goddamn done with his training, a little bit of starvation will toughen him up," he said.

Mommy again shrank back against the window. Dad continued, a little bit more calmly now. "Men are great conquerors, son! We take whatever it is we want, whenever it is we want it, and if something stands in your way, you knock it down! That goes for both on *and* off the field, son. Life, for us men, is all about going on the offense. Defense will only keep you behind the line, but offense will take you where it is you want to go."

"Yes, Dad, I will try harder next week, and I will practice more," I said, looking him straight in the eyes in the mirror. That was one thing Dad valued highly, flawed as it was. He assumed people were telling the truth if they looked you straight in the eyes. So, unless he happened to be in a particularly ornery mood, compliance and submission were usually the best tactics to use. Dad began to breathe normally again, and the pulsing in his temple slowed.

We pulled up into our driveway and I immediately hopped out of the car to go do my penance. I heard Mommy and my sister get out of the car behind me, and then Dad say something as he drove away. Off to the bar no doubt.

Dad hadn't always been like this. He had always been a "macho-man," sure, and had even served in the Army after the terrorist attack on the Twin Towers. But it had just been over the past year that he had grown so constantly angry at *everything*. Last spring, Dad's friend from the Army had killed himself.

I still remember the beer on Dad's breath coming all the way across the kitchen table as he corrected Mommy's soft-spoken "Your father's friend from the Army passed away."

"He didn't fucking pass away!" Dad yelled at her. "He was a fucking coward that couldn't handle it, and he blew his own head off. He took the pussy way out..." Bits of turkey flew out of his mouth as he hit the P in pussy, and he ignored them, leaving them there for Mom to clean up later.

My sister and I looked at Dad with bewilderment. This was the first we were hearing about someone, anyone, taking their own life. We didn't know what to think.

"He was no man, and no friend of mine. Not anymore. Only a pussy leaves his wife and son to suffer like that. See how lucky you guys are? I will never leave you..." He was trying to sound sincere, but what came out was much more ominous.

After Dad's "training camp" that I had gone through before the season started, it didn't take me very long to do my exercises that night, and I was soon sitting at the dinner table with Mommy and my sister. Mommy had kept my plate warm. My fried chicken was still crispy, just the way I like it.

For a long time, we sat in silence and ate our dinner. All three of us examining our days, and each questioning how we could better please Dad. Mommy was the first to break the silence as she turned to my sister. "You were just perfect in your halftime performance, sweetie, you did an excellent job." She turned to me. "I saw you when you blocked that big boy so that he wouldn't score! You did a great job too!" She smiled at us both, and we smiled back and thanked her, but Mommy's smiles never seemed real. They always seemed like the shadow of a smile, or an imposter. Never genuine.

"I tripped on that play," I admitted. "The guy only fell because his feet got tangled up in me as I went down. I didn't tackle him."

Mommy looked at me, and this time smiled her real, genuine smile, the one we never got to see anymore, and said, "Sometimes some of our greatest mistakes can have the happiest of endings." She got up and hugged us both before beginning to clear the table.

My sister and I helped Mommy with the dishes and then went off to plug away at our homework. Well, I was *supposed* to be doing my homework, but I had made other plans. I quietly closed my bedroom door, then turned on my radio to my favorite classical music station, and retrieved my sketchpad from its secret hiding place.

I had to keep it hidden from Dad because he said that "drawing was for sissies," but I really loved to draw. My sketchpad was filled with all sorts of cool stuff I had seen: sunsets, trees, rocks, cars, animals, and bugs. Bugs had always been my favorite.

That morning while I was brushing my teeth, a big brown spider had crawled out of the sink drain. I bent down on my stool and stared at him as he attempted to climb up the side of the slippery porcelain. Time and time again he tumbled down the slick basin back towards the drain.

I pulled the plug that closed the drain and ran back to my room to retrieve my special bug jar, the one with a magnifying glass in the lid. I ran back to the bathroom and deftly swept the spider into my container. I had stuck the jar in my desk for after school, and I had hoped all day that he wouldn't get out before I could draw him.

Now, I retrieved my new friend and was happy to see he was still there. He was even still alive. I put the jar on my bed and sat cross-legged with my pad on my lap. He was a bit too willing to sit still and sometimes I had to shake him up a little to get him to move so that I could get a better look at the other parts of him. He was a lot smoother than most of the spiders around here, so I didn't have to spend much time drawing all of the tiny hair, which was a relief.

I had waited all day to get back to him. I had even been thinking about drawing during the football game, which had made me miss that pass. I'd had spiders on the brain all day. I couldn't help it. I loved drawing and animals. I did not love sports.

I couldn't get his abdomen quite right and it was bothering me. The square jar didn't offer a very good view of the spider's side so I shook him again, but still couldn't get him to move the way I wanted him to.

He wasn't all that big, and I figured that I could always squash him if I really needed to, so I freed my spider friend and let him out on my bed. He didn't move for the next five minutes, allowing me to get a very good look at him. He started to crawl away just as I was putting the finishing touches on the drawing. He moved slowly at first, then picked up speed as he neared the edge of the blanket, and I instinctively moved my leg to block him from falling off the bed.

The spider jumped at my movement, which in turn made *me* jump in surprise, and he became lost in a flurry of sheets and blankets as I scrambled out of bed. I didn't know where he'd gone. I couldn't see him anywhere on the floor, so I assumed he was still in the bed.

One by one, I slowly peeled back the layers of my bedding, waiting for the spider to jump out at me again. When the sheet was removed and the bed was fully exposed, the spider was nowhere to be found. I shrugged and figured we'd just go back to living our separate lives. At least I got a good look at him, so I sat back down to add a bit more shading to my drawing.

Only then did I realize where he'd gone as I felt him bite me right in the thigh, just below my butt. I felt a stab that sent me reeling off the bed again. When I stood, his crumpled little body fell out of my shorts, one leg still twitching like he was waving goodbye.

The bite hadn't hurt that much, and there was only a dull pain, so I ignored it. I just hoped it would be gone before our next game on Wednesday. Dad would be very mad if I couldn't play.

I scooped the spider back into the jar and took it to the bathroom. I tossed him in the toilet and waved my own goodbye as the swirling water took him. The pain seemed to lessen as I walked back to my room, and I lay on my belly and did my actual schoolwork until bedtime. I heard Dad come home just as I was drifting off to sleep. There wasn't any yelling, so hopefully he wasn't mad at me anymore.

*

The pain woke me up before anyone else. I opened my eyes to find them blurry with tears. But my entire body hurt from yesterday's game, so I didn't really pay attention to the more intense throbbing in my thigh. I carefully got dressed and went downstairs. Dad was sleeping on the couch and he awoke as I crept into the kitchen.

"Ahhhh, why do you always have to be so damn loud?" Dad yelled. He threw the blanket off and sat up. He rubbed his temples, stretched, and stood up to punch me in my arm as he passed me on his way to take a shower. My shoulder always hurt from him doing this; I had a constant bruise, but it meant he was in an OK mood, so I let it go.

I was limping around the kitchen when Mommy came in. "Did you get hurt yesterday?" she said and grabbed me by the hand while looking me over.

"No, Mommy, my muscles are just a bit sore, I'll be OK. I'm tough!" I told her.

Dad heard this and came back in. "He's going to have to be sore until he works up anything that comes close to resembling muscle. He's weak, and has to suffer through some pain in order to get stronger. He'll be alright. I sure came out OK!"

I wondered why people who say they "came out OK" never really seem to have come out OK. I realized Dad was looking at me.

"Ugh, yeah, Mommy, I'll be fine. What doesn't kill me will make me stronger, isn't that right, Dad? I just gotta man up!"

"That's right, son," he said to me, and then turned and smiled at Mommy. Nothing more to be said.

Dad dropped me off at my school on his way to work. He didn't speak to me on the way there, he mostly just yelled at other drivers and at talk radio. My leg was hurting much more by the time we arrived. I hopped out of the car without showing any pain, and I said goodbye to Dad. He barely acknowledged me as he drove off.

I limped first to the bathroom to have a look in front of one of the big mirrors. The bite was about the size of a golf ball and it was pretty red, but I figured it should shrink down before the next game. The creak of the door made me pull up my pants quickly as I heard other students coming into the bathroom. I tried not to think much about it the rest of the day. It hurt, but I just had to "play through the pain" like Daddy would say.

It wasn't any better when I got home, and Mommy noticed me limping again. She went to the cupboard and pulled out the bottle of children's Tylenol. She gave me two big spoonfuls (before Dad got home from work so that he wouldn't know) and it really helped, so the spider bite was soon forgotten by a game of hide-and-seek with my sister.

It hurt a lot worse on Tuesday. I was having trouble walking, but I was able to sneak some more medicine before school. I was sweating all the time and I was starting to feel pretty weak. By Wednesday, I was so tired that Mommy had a hard time waking me up for school and suggested that I may have to stay home and miss the game.

Dad yelled at her, "Goddamn it! How many times do I have to say this shit? He will never become a man if you don't stop fucking coddling him! You're reversing everything I've tried to accomplish with *my* son." He glared at her, challenging her to challenge him.

When she didn't, he turned to me, and said, "A big part of becoming a man is playing the game while hurt, son. This is the point that separates the boys from the men. We play when we're hurt or sick, we play hard, and we play no matter what! You're no coward, right?" He punched my shoulder.

"Right, Dad!" I managed, reaching up to give him a meager high five, and then shooting Mommy an "I'm fine" look, while I rubbed my shoulder.

Dad drove me to school again, and when we got there, I went to take another look at the spider bite. It was really bad. It was a lot bigger than the day before and it was turning black. I also think it smelled funny, but that could have just been the bathroom.

I slowly shuffled to class, stopping only when passing by the new mural that was being painted. I leaned against the lockers and listened to a group of teachers talking about the mural. They were saying that it would "do the girl justice," and hopefully bring some "change to the long-running systematic injustices," whatever that meant. What had made me stop was the little girl's face. It was very familiar to me.

I had heard the story when other kids talked about it, but I never knew what the girl had looked like before. She had been about my age, and she'd been walking home from this same school. It had been her birthday, and she'd stopped at the creek to throw rocks in the water. She was minding her own business, reading a book, when she'd been beaten and killed by some teenagers because she was Black.

It didn't make sense to me, any of it. But I was sure that I knew her somehow, even though she had died before I was born. I stood there, leaning against the wall, and stared into the girl's eyes. So familiar. "Tiffany's Law" was all it said. The tardy bell jerked me back to reality and I made my way slowly and painfully to class.

I thought I must have a fever because I was very very shaky, but I had to man up, or else. My thigh felt like it was on fire, and it was definitely the bite that smelled. The horrible stench had followed me throughout the day. Even at lunch where I thought the smell of food would overpower it, I could still smell it. It smelled like the dead rat I had found once. But I knew that men had to ignore pain.

After school that day, I went and dressed in my pads and uniform. I hobbled out onto the field with the rest of my team, because "we don't ever let down our team." I was grateful for the helmet, as it hid my tears as I ran, play after play.

I was able to cover up my sobs under the guise of being out of breath, for the most part. I played on as the pain crept into me further, the increased blood flow helping the venom along its way. But I was doing it! We were winning the game! I was playing through my pain, I was becoming a man, and I was making my dad proud!

We were already ahead by a good amount, even though the points didn't matter, so they decided to pass the ball to me. They only did this by accident, or when failure was no longer possible. It was to be a short pass, just enough to get us into the end zone one last time to seal the opposition's fate.

The play went well enough. I ran through the agony, and the ball sailed easily into my grasp. I ran, until my leg came down and was greeted by the spider bite's necrosis, crumpling the muscle just as the largest kid on the other team came my way. The boy slammed into me with a force that I had only ever felt from my Dad's backhand.

Sparks burst into my vision as I was knocked unconscious and regained my "being" simultaneously.

The sound of my snapping spine was overpowered by the flashing visions of every single birth that had ever taken place on Earth. The venom that coursed through my veins was but a memory compared to the unfolding evolution of all flower-life that I was currently witnessing. The sounds of the game hollowing until silent, making way for the cracking and shaking of great tectonic mountains being formed as I watched.

I was whole once again. I was filled with the love and compassion of the entire world, and I was ready to begin my mission anew. But my new little body was not, and it lay unconscious and twitching on the field.

Time became indiscernible with the boy in a coma. How long I floated, I don't know. It felt like years. The boy's body had been horribly ravaged by the spider's venom, and the broken back had only distracted the doctor's attention. They hadn't noticed the decaying tissue or the smell at first, and by the time they did, it was too late for the little boy.

The venom entered the bloodstream as he ran, and the darling little boy had died from a heart attack at his father's behest...

This was all sorts of wrong! The whole process was changing completely, and I wasn't even being allowed to begin to attempt my mission. It was infuriating. The mural came to mind.

She had been me. I was that girl. They had killed me, just as I had found myself again. Nathan and the bus driver coming together, this boy's dad serving in the war with Jacob's dad... These types of connections had not been possible before – they couldn't be. There simply wasn't an Earthly mechanism in place that would allow for it. But yet, here they were.

Why were these ones so different? Why were they painting a mural? Why was I being murdered? The questions hung unanswered as I floated in limbo between the two parts of *the whole*.

I didn't want to go anywhere. I wanted to just float here in my limbo, but I couldn't even do that right. I felt myself being pulled back to our pool, as I wept for the abused that never even get their chance.

*

In our light, surrounded by our collective energy, I was finally given the chance to piece my recent lives together.

With the looming darkness I had to think fast. There had been no real time for reflection in between these lives; that had never happened before. My lives now seemed to be connecting in certain places, at certain times. Possibly I had simply been a necessary presence.

I had been killed directly after learning of my purpose in all three lives, and that had never happened before. Certainly not three in a row. This last time, I had changed really early in the boy's life, almost as if it was before he was ready. That had only happened that *one* time before…

The mural had said "law," which means that Tiffany's life and death had created widespread change. Had these intertwined lives been forced so that the needed changes could be set in motion? Can they all be a part of some grand scheme?

Deep energy pulses from the pool suggested that I was definitely onto something with these thoughts.

Great evolution was taking place amid *the whole*, I could definitely feel *that*. Each life had been an extreme example of the forces of racism, religious hypocrisy, and a toxic patriarchy. The path for Us was in constant competition against these things, and we were losing. These are some of the most grievous affronts to the very nature of our being. If *the whole* is forcing change, there may be an even greater need for my message. My timeframes have been sped up, the Earth begs to be healed; it's time to kick some ass!

I gather what strength I can, steady my resolve, and with a renewed sense of purpose, I am tossed into those varying degrees of childhood circumstance. Only now, hopefully, in a time of great striving progress, my message will not only be actively searched for out of necessity, but also may be much more easily received. Chaos and strife are the precursors of great change.

I grit my teeth with resolute purpose, and I plunge.

Chapter 5

I became aware only to find myself still surrounded by my mother. I was floating in my own personal bath of amniotic fluid. My small stomach gurgled with hunger. I could hear the constant drumming of her heartbeat under the undersea-like noises of the rest of her, and I could feel our blood pulsing through my veins. Her emotions, thoughts, and fears were my own. Our two separate energies functioned as one.

She was scared. Her heart beat faster than normal. The surges of adrenaline made my small appendages twitch and spasm. I felt her start to hurry and the surge worsened. One strong twitch of my leg hit the side of the womb, and I could feel Mom double over in pain, but she recovered, and we continued on. Soon, she was all but running. I was sloshing about in my soggy cocoon. I could feel her reasoning. She had to get home before he did, or he was going to be angry. She had to have dinner on the table every night by seven. We reached the bus stop and we could rest. Before long, we heard the loud hiss of a bus pulling up. It was loud enough for me to hear over the sound-dampening womb, and we felt relief flow into us. We had made it. "Good job, Mom, sorry I kicked you!" I thought, and was rewarded with rubs as she sat down.

Now we were tired, and we hoped the bus wouldn't break down. We bounced in our seat with the bus's progression, and it was not long before the jolts made Mom have to pee. "Of course!" she said aloud, and she began to cry.

We couldn't very well wet ourselves, especially when we had plenty of notice to get off and use a bathroom, but then we would be late getting home. We hopped off at the next stop and hoped that he wouldn't be on time coming home from work. We hurried to a nearby convenience store and begged the cashier for the key, promising to buy something on the way out.

We hurried back outside and around to the bathroom. Disgust hit us as the acrid stench of old urine and feces wafted into Mom's nose. But her bladder gave us no choice and we made a dash inside. We wished we could at least leave the door open, but we locked it behind us for safety. Our heartbeat slowed as she held her breath and "hovered" over the toilet, and my space increased as she peed. We didn't even wash as we left, opting for hand sanitizer from her purse, and we ran back into the store to return the key.

"Aren't you going to buy anything? You promised," the young woman behind the counter called as we turned to leave.

I kicked Mom again. Not on purpose, but a kick of reflex in response to my hunger. She answered by rubbing her tummy to soothe me, and she whispered, "OK, OK. I will see what they have here. We can eat it on the ride home. I'm sure nobody will pester the pregnant lady about food on the bus if we're clean about it."

We stopped at the door. "Of course," Mom said to the cashier, and we turned back to find something quick to purchase. The influx of hormones was affecting her memory. Lapses were becoming more and more common, and he had started making fun of her for it.

She looked through the rows and rows of junk food in order to find something suitable for me. The food here was mostly filled with dyes and preservatives. Mom quickly paced the aisle looking through the hundreds of different types of chips. She eventually found a bag of popcorn that looked to be relatively free of "extras" and we took it up to pay for it.

As we handed over our card, Mom saw a bottle up on a shelf behind the counter. It was his favorite vodka, and she thought that showing up with that in hand might make up for our lateness.

"I'll also take that bottle, please," Mom said, and the girl rung it up. She eyeballed Mom's swollen belly as she did, and Mom quickly added, "It's not for us, don't worry." We put our card back into our purse, thanked the woman, and ran back to the bus stop.

Our ride came quickly, and Mom was offered a window seat by a gentleman who tipped his Indiana Jones hat at us as he passed by. We thanked him, and sat down with a huff. Mom wiggled and repositioned herself until she found the most comfortable way to sit, which happened to be staring out the window.

As the city blocks passed by, Mom wished to be home. Not the apartment where we lived here, but back in her childhood home. With Mom's father's salary as a surgeon, her parents had been able to purchase a hundred acres of prime California land when she and her sister were still young. The rolling hills were dotted with wildflowers in the spring and tall wavy grasses in the summer, and the house that she'd grown up in was painted to match. The girls spent their youth climbing trees, rustling all manners of critters, swimming in the pond, and having campouts. All in their own backyard. It was a paradise that she had taken for granted.

Mom had never liked the busyness of the city, even though she had grown more accustomed to it. She was used to lazy ranch days and the quiet solitude of nature, certainly not this perpetual collectiveness of human activity. Mom was not happy, and she quietly cried the rest of the way.

We were home in under twenty minutes, just enough time to work up another pee. We peeked around the corner before we got to the door, and saw that the parking spot was empty! He wasn't here!

We made it to our own bathroom and right after, we washed more thoroughly to remove the *other* bathroom. We put his bottle in the freezer to chill, and we took off our bra. Mom's breasts had started to engorge, and had grown quite painful in the past few weeks. Plus, going braless might help to lighten the mood, should he get home before dinner was ready. We rushed to start cooking.

As we gathered the ingredients from the cupboard, Mom turned on the small television that sat on the counter next to the stand-mixer. It was an old TV, probably nearing thirty years old. Its black-and-white screen was only about three inches square, and was backed up by about a foot of plastic hardware containment. It had been her father's garage TV, and it still gave off a faint smell of car grease as it first warmed up.

The picture slowly grew outward from a tiny glowing dot in the middle of the screen, and there was an electrical whine that faded as the screen filled with the snow of poor reception. The speaker crackled as a program fought to come through, and Mom turned the small antenna in various directions until both picture and sound were clear. We resumed our dinner-prep-dance as the TV provided a much-needed distraction.

"…*and be sure not to miss out our world-famous beaches and luxurious resorts here in Sandals Jamaica! Where the island becomes you.*"

We started to cut up the vegetables for the stuffing as the commercial segment came to an end, and the evening news program resumed its broadcast.

"Welcome back, viewers. In tonight's local news spot, we have a tragic story coming out of the youth sports arena. A peewee football player has passed away overnight after he sustained substantial injuries while on the field. The young boy had been in a coma after his back was broken during a routine game, and he eventually succumbed to his injuries late last night. Further investigation into the boy's death may occur, but first, the child's father reached out to our newsroom looking to make a statement. So we will now go live to our very own Chad Harrington, who is with the child's father now. Chad?"

"Thank you, Bill. Yes, a community is in mourning today as the grim news of the child's death spread. Small vigils like this one that you see behind me have been popping up all over town, as the people of this small suburb attempt to find some expression for their grief.

"With me now is the boy's father. Sir, what thoughts do you wish to share with our viewers?"

"Are we live? Am I on live TV? Um, yeah. I just wanted to talk about my boy. I wanted to tell the world just how strong my boy was, so that they can find their own strength if they need to. Um… This is really live? Wow. Um, my boy loved to play football. He wanted to make his daddy proud, so he tried his best. I guess sometimes even our best just isn't enough… Um, and I wanted to thank everyone for the support and attention everybody has given me in this time of sadness. I know my boy is up in heaven right now, playing catch with the Big Guy. Thank you."

We reached over and turned off the TV in disgust. "Despicable!" Mom said aloud. "What a horrible, wretched human being! His son isn't even cold yet, and he's out here talking to the camera like his team had just won the Stanley Cup. Absolutely appalling." Mom was getting frustrated, and we could feel my tiny heartbeat increasing.

Mom sat for a moment and took a few big breaths to settle down. With her hormones out of whack, she sometimes had to physically control her body by resigning herself to slow and even breathing. When we had calmed down, we resumed making dinner in silence.

We were just about elbow deep into the raw chicken, attempting to retrieve the final piece of gizzard that had lodged itself in a crevice, when we heard the garage door begin to whir and we froze. "Shit!" Mom said aloud. Panic. Fear. Anxiety. He was home, and we were not done with dinner.

We turned towards the door and put on our best "I love you, sorry I messed up" demeanor. We were just crossing our fingers that he'd had a good day at work when he bustled into the kitchen through the garage door. His mood couldn't be discerned. He wasn't yelling, but he wasn't smiling either. He set his lunch box down and looked towards the table, which wasn't set. He sniffed the air, and when he smelled nothing, he grunted. "No dinner tonight, eh, woman?"

"You can plainly see this bird stuck on my hand; we were a little late coming home," Mom said.

With that, she rubbed me with her free hand, making sure he remembered that I was still there. "There was trouble with the bus," she lied, "and we had to stop real fast to pee, but we picked up a little something for you when we stopped. It's in the freezer. Please go easy on it."

We motioned with the chicken and he grumbled his way over to the fridge. The grumbles shifted to delight when he saw what was in the freezer, and he grabbed a glass. He tossed a few ice cubes into the cup with a clink, and then he was off to his man cave without another word.

It wasn't much of a man cave, but he had turned the little storage room connected to their apartment porch into his "study," as he called it. Where other people used the space to store boxes or recycling, he had stuck an old desk in there and a cheap laptop. Every night he would come home and go out there to drink beer, smoke cheap cigars, and to rant about his older brother Nathan. Nathan had recently run for the Senate and won, and was now spearheading a law that would effectively outlaw racism. We were proud of Nathan.

Mom's husband, however, had nothing but resentment for his younger brother. Nathan's success infuriated him, and he would go on long drunken tirades about how their parents used to dote on the younger child, leaving the older to "fend for scraps" as he put it. It was creepy to see someone so obsessed with another's success... Nights were now filled with him yelling at his brother's face as he was featured on various prominent news programs. When it would go quiet, we would go out to find him passed out in his own filth, and would then have to help him to bed. But for now, he had gone to his study without so much as a thank-you. Things were OK though, things were OK at the moment.

We were feeling a bit better. He had what he needed, and we went to work finishing dinner. It took longer than we thought it would, about an hour or so, but the chicken looked just about perfect as we placed it on the table among the other dishes of mashed potatoes, gravy, his mother's baked bean casserole, and a secret pie we had found in the back of the freezer. We had stuck it in the oven just after taking out the chicken. It was peach, our favorite, not his, but hopefully it would do.

We called to him as we lit a candle, and we even smiled at how good the food looked. We heard him get up, and saw his shadow darken the sliding door as he rose from his hovel. He took a first step and stumbled. We could see the bottle glisten in the moonlight as he raised it to his lips. We watched in astonishment as he slowly drained the few remaining swallows in great heaving gulps, and he turned and pitched the empty bottle against the side of the neighboring apartment with a loud crash. Luckily, the apartment had recently been vacated. He almost fell through the big glass door with the backward momentum of the throw, only barely catching the frame of the slider. He turned and came inside, and for a moment, he so seemingly helpless in his drunken stupor, a touch of pity ran through us.

That pity changed the instant we saw his glazed-over eyes. They were bloodshot, giving him a devilish quality, but there was so much more. Below the broken capillaries and glaze we saw hate. His eyes said death.

He growled: a sickening sound that made us want to run. He lurched at us, and we were barely able to dodge his clawing hand, but he backed us further into our small kitchen. We were frozen with terror. Our blood was racing, and we knew we had to get out.

We tried. We fought back for once, but he was so much stronger. He pinned us in the corner of the kitchen and began pummeling us. He screamed in our face between blows, telling us how worthless we were, how pathetic, and how we could never be a good mother if we couldn't even get a simple dinner ready on time.

We kicked and bit him, but his punches didn't stop, and our eyes began to swell, making it hard to see. We felt ashamed, guilty, angry, and sorry, but our body felt only agony.

It took us a second to realize the attack had stopped. We continued to twitch in fear as if the blows were still falling, but he had stumbled away. He was gone. We heard the front door slam, and his footsteps made the whole apartment vibrate as we heard him sway and pitch down the front stairs. He was gone. We lay there cowering, unable to move as we listened and assured ourselves that he was truly gone.

The smells of pie and chicken were still lingering, and they still smelled the same, but their odor was making us sick. We shook as we sat up and leaned against the cabinet. The kitchen was a mess. Broken plates and silverware skittered across the floor as we forced our arms to move. We raised our hands to Mom's face, and they came away covered in red, though we could only just make them out through the tears and swelling. We grabbed the oven door handle and tried to stand, but our feet weren't willing, and the handle broke off completely in our hand.

Defeated and unsteady, amid our own pooling blood, we started to crawl to the bathroom. The shards of broken crockery cut us as we pulled ourselves along, but we didn't care.

We passed the perfect chicken, smashed on the floor. The carpet would have to be cleaned. We saw that he had knocked over the bookshelf in the hallway. It leaned against the opposite wall, its contents in a heap underneath. We tried to push the books out of the way, but we gave up and climbed over them. It took almost all of our remaining strength, but we eventually pulled ourselves into the bathroom.

Then, with one final heave, we were able to hoist ourselves into a standing position at the vanity. We closed the door behind us, not that it would do much good if he came back. It was more hole than door after he'd punched it so many times. We left behind smeared bloody fingerprints as we turned the fake porcelain handles and the water in the sink turned a dark red. Blood seemed to be flowing from everywhere at once but eventually we were able to raise our head to meet the gaze in the mirror.

There were many deep cuts, most still bleeding. The largest was on our forehead. It seemed to have been caused by his class ring, and was gushing a river of blood down the channels of Mom's nose.

It was at this sight, this particular vision, that I felt her break. Her battered body closely followed by her battered soul. The reflection of herself pushed her past her limits, past *most* people's limits, and we... changed. Her will left us. She could no longer do this, and she could only see one way out. She could not bear a child and live with this man, as he would certainly make it his mission to turn the child into a monster. It was OK, I was her, and I understood.

I understood when we wiped our eyes, and I understood when those eyes noticed the dress hanger on the back of the door. I understood, as Mom understood. It was hard to reach, our muscles starting to seize up from the tension, but with effort we were able to grab it. I understood.

We both sobbed as Mom untwisted the metal hanger, exposing its cork-screwed end. We understood that there are times in life where people can no longer accept suffering, that rape victims should not have to bear their attacker's child. That women can have too many children, and not wish to have anymore. That there are many imperative reasons for a woman to have to make such a horrendous decision, and that that decision is hers alone. These were both of our thoughts and understandings.

But Mom was missing something, something that I alone could pass on to her, and I did. I felt the great tides of joy rise with her understanding, as she now knew, too. She knew that we all would return to the energy pool, one way or another. That we each are our own puzzle pieces, and our mission is to find where we fit in *the whole*. Mom wasn't scared anymore, and we gave in.

Battered, broken, and bereft, Mom slid to the floor and struggled with her underwear. We understood. Wire in hand, she inserted the sharp hanger into herself and started thrusting, but we understood.

We understood as it pierced our flesh, time and time again. We understood. We understood as Mom got careless in her efforts, and one of her stabs missed its mark, only to rupture one of her arteries. We understood.

We lay there, bleeding, but with great relief. It would be over. Mom would not have to suffer any longer. She would be released from her prison, and we would go to the pool. We understood. We were not scared anymore.

The blood ran out for both of us. Its weakening pulse but a whisper, as we dissipated into nothing, into everything. Mom and I became all.

*

The pool was electrified with the friction of combat. The darkness was noticeable, and the conflict between light and dark was the source of the noise. I could feel the weakened pool as it barely released its energy in its attempts to fill me. The sanctuary had grown terribly dark, and I was not able to fully recharge. Weakness and fury are not a good combination.

Mom still clung to my root being, not wanting to let go. Small bits of her floated away, and I even saw one bit turn to black, but most of her stayed right by me. I urged her to go, to help fight the invader while I was gone, but she would not leave me. She was tenacious.

She began to shine brighter, and her being held its form as it began pulsing in tandem with my own. We were there, in complete sync with one another, two distinct beings acting as one, and then she swarmed me with her energy.

To my surprise, Mom gave herself completely to the cause. The bits of the void that had taken up residence in me were no longer there. Mom selflessly released any semblance of herself, and she gave me the truest gift. Our energy became one. We joined our power-rings like in the old comic books, and through her action I was able to become whole once again.

The strangeness of the past life didn't change my determination, and neither did the impending darkness. If anything, it reasserted my true calling. Humans *would* heed my message, or their actions *would* lead to their own undoing.

Shit, I could show these fuckers if I wanted to. I could give up on them and come back as a tree. Have myself a go at advanced sentience in forest form. That would show 'em! And I really did have a greater fondness for trees now, after Jacob. I could drop branches and shit down on their stupid heads. Just up and split in half to scare the pants off of 'em. Ooo, I could make everything poisonous and itchy!

But not yet. I had to do what I could for *the whole* before it was too late. Mom and I donned the war paint of our unity. This might be the very last chance for humanity, so our battle cry of *"FOR TACOS!"* was murderous as Mom and I plunged back into the Earthly fray.

Chapter 6

I grew up in a suburb of Tulsa, Oklahoma. Farm country. There, I weathered my youth by burying myself in schoolbooks and playing as much stickball as a boy possibly could.

I was the middle child, and had an older brother and younger twin sisters for siblings. Dad was an accountant for a law firm in the city, and Mom was a housewife. We had a modest house, with the typical white picket fence and a tire swing, and we all fit pretty well into suburban life.

As kids, our summers were spent on the various family farms with our aunts and uncles and our many cousins. We were up with the roosters, milking, chores, hay baling, and feeding the livestock. This was stuff I didn't get at home, and such work was supposed to keep me rounded. But once the chores were done for the day, we had free rein to do almost anything we wanted.

Most of my extracurriculars revolved around animals. I had a soft spot for almost all of God's creatures, but the ones that the girls deemed "gross" were certainly my favorite, as they always got such great reactions.

My sisters were used to my shenanigans, having to put up with them year-round, but during the summer, my female cousins would become fresh meat, and I would torture them with whatever animals I could find.

One hot and muggy day when I was ten years old, me and my cousin Clyde were chasing a small whip snake through the long underbrush. Clyde had swung around in front of the little fella trying to cut him off, but the snake just doubled back towards me.

I was quick, and I deftly grabbed it behind its head, so he couldn't get a tooth or two in. The snake was harmless enough, but it still smarted when we got bit.

Clyde offered me the little burlap sack we always carried for just this occasion, and I lowered our prize inside. Tying it shut, Clyde found a stick and hung the bag from it, and swung the stick onto his shoulder like a hobo. We smiled at each other.

We headed back home, kicking at the grass as we went to see if we could rustle up a few more snakes. Our search was fruitless as we only managed to scare a few quail who took flight ahead of us. But it was all right. One single snake held an immense amount of power, and this one would do just fine for our purposes.

The day before, Clyde's sisters had lured us out onto the back porch, claiming there was a huge tarantula that needed to be squashed right away. Ruth had stood there screaming and pointing behind an old wooden box, making quite a fuss. Barbara didn't appear until a few moments later when Clyde and I bent down to examine the spot where the spider was supposed to be.

Up from the second-story window came the whoosh of water falling, when the day's dirty laundry leavings were tossed onto our unsuspecting heads.

Soggy and grimy, we angrily chased after Ruth. The odor of dirt and soap filled the yard as we ran. Clyde paused the chase for a moment to chuck a rock up Barbara's way. He only narrowly missed the pane of glass as she slammed the window shut, and stuck her tongue out at us from behind it.

We never did catch Ruth or Barbara, but we hatched a plan for revenge.

On Wednesdays, the girls had their piano lessons. During these lessons, they would begin by warming up together, attempting to play scales in harmony. The piano wasn't fancy, but it had been in the family for generations. It was made from highly polished oak and was soft to the touch. It stood upright in the far corner of my aunt and uncle's parlor, and aside from a sizable crack along the top where something had fallen onto it long ago, the piano was in great condition.

The girls were still having their pre-lesson tea party out on the lawn, all dressed up with their dolls. They didn't see the two of us sneak into the parlor and stash our ophidian prize inside the piano. Clyde and I hid behind the couch in the parlor just as the girls came jostling in. They were still giggly from their very fancy pretend soiree. They sat down on the piano bench and removed their lace gloves to begin their sheet-music lessons.

As the two began smashing the piano keys in attempted unison (they really were *not* very good), Clyde and I poked our heads out from behind either side of the couch to watch our trick unfurl.

The snake, agitated by the musical number, quickly found its way to the crack and out of the piano lid. It began slithering along the top of the instrument looking for the best place to hide, jerking in response to all the noise.

The girls didn't look up to see it, but Clyde and I had to stifle our giggles behind the couch. The poor snake, finding the edge of the lid, changed direction and raced back to the middle, desperately looking for a way off.

There was only one way to go and the snake sat coiled in the center of the lid looking ready to strike.

For a moment, it appeared like he was going to sit there, unmoving. But then, the noise became too much and he reared back and launched himself at the reading light the girls used to illuminate their sheet music.

Thankfully, the snake missed. Our serpent friend landed directly on a series of keys, adding a third contributor to the cacophony.

His tail landed on Barbara's hand and the loud screaming began. Both girls jumped up, knocking over the piano bench with a great crash, and they ran wailing from the room. They cried out to the heavens about an anaconda as our gales of laughter followed after them.

This was me to a T. Always in on the joke, and most often the cause of it. Times were different back then. During my teenage years, I caught a serious bug. Not the average flu or cold, but the travel bug. Wanderlust. I needed to see more of what the world had to offer. I needed to better understand the greatness this country was supposed to provide.

Back in the forties and fifties, there were no real qualms about hitchhiking. One could simply pack up a bag, walk through their front door down, and stick out a thumb. Some neighbor would eventually pass by on their way to the store and they'd give you a ride. Many boys back then were able to travel all over the country, mostly for free, because the times seemed to be safer than they are now.

My own thumbs took me west, as the fabled California lifestyle appealed to me. I could go and learn to surf like they did in the movies. I could attend some beach blanket bonanzas, and I could even go all the way to Hollywood. Who knew? The sky was the limit.

I made it to just over the Nevada border in about two weeks, all the way to Yosemite National Park. It was there that I stopped to rest in this place of tremendous beauty. Loving what I saw, I decided to inquire about a job.

The summer was just beginning and employment was very scarce during this busy season, but I was in luck. A busboy had just caught a bad case of poison oak while hiking and they were in desperate need of someone to take his place.

The guy never ended up returning to the job, so it became mine, and oh boy did I love it! We were so busy. We worked sixty hours a week, sometimes more, but they also had us on a rotating work schedule so that after two weeks every group of workers got a four-day weekend. These times were epic!

Big groups of us would hike to the remotest points of the park, driving to certain points if need be, and we would spend our days off "lost" in some of the best wilderness the Earth has to offer. We drank and partied and generally had a gay ole time.

We awoke to herds of deer having their breakfast just out of reach of our tents. We dove mostly naked off granite cliffs amid pure falls, just for the thrill of it. We ran through the brush with wild foxes and screamed our troubles away into the treetops. We were the kings and queens of the forest, and we ruled it all.

Then we went back to reality and back to our work as grunts for another two weeks. Although the job was strenuous, it was a teenager's dream and I spent the entire summer in the blissful fog of youth.

As the season came to a close, I made the decision not to return home. A king of the forest could not return to a suburb.

The summer was ending, but that meant college was going to be starting soon. I made it to San Francisco within a few days, and then I figured out how to put myself on the waiting list for enrolment at UCSF.

I got a job as a gas jockey at the Sinclair station not far from campus, which allowed me to rent a room and feed myself. I didn't know how I would pay for school, but I saved what I could as I waited and studied.

During my wait, I found that I could sneak into the university library using groups of students as cover. Once inside, I could read to my heart's content. By the time I was notified that I'd been accepted, the entrance exams were no problem.

I met my wife at the university. Ellen went to an all-girl sister-school nearby, and she and I were both part of the joint University Naturalist Group. This group would take students on hikes and bird-watching excursions, and we'd go on extended camping trips outside of the area. Ellen and I bonded over our mutual love of animals, and we were married in a quaint ceremony before we graduated.

We ended up deciding that I would continue with my studies and get my doctorate degree, and she would start her career as a teacher in order to support us. Ellen found a job as a kindergarten teacher and I went to med school.

Before I could become the orthopedic surgeon I would eventually be, our family grew. We had our first daughter in my second year of medical school, and then our second daughter was born just before I earned the title of doctor. Our two children became our whole lives, and Ellen and I decided that the city wasn't the proper environment in which to raise them.

After a few years of searching, and after I had become fairly established in my field, we finally found what we were looking for in the foothills of the Sacramento Valley.

There, hidden behind the rolling hills, dotted with live oak, we found our home. The hills were covered in yellowed dry grasses that waved in the wind, and game trails weaved through the great tufts. Huge flocks of small birds twisted and turned in the sky, chasing swarms of bugs. A stream ran down from the hills and meandered through the property before feeding a large pond. The pond was alive with tadpoles and water skimmers, and a young turtle sunned itself on an old log. Beneath a few rocks were some alligator lizards and one fat old corn snake that slowly wandered into the brush. This part of the Earth called to our very being. It was a paradise for us alone.

We bought the land, and moved our small family into the tiny cottage that had been left in disrepair. The roof leaked come wintertime, but it was warm and cozy, and it was our home while the plans were being drawn up for more spacious accommodations. Our girls loved it, as their backyard was a hundred acres of open hills in which to wander and play. Ellen loved it because of the variety of birds that flittered around, and I loved it because it was ours.

I set up my business in a nearby city and began practicing medicine. Here, I became known for my intricate work, and I took on many patients through the San Francisco sports teams, even though I was some eighty miles away from the city. This not only boosted my practice, but it hurried our house plans along.

Soon, our brand-new home was complete, elegantly awash in the morning sun among the green grasses and rolling hills. It was a bit larger than we needed because the children were not yet fully grown, but Ellen and I anticipate grandchildren someday, and we could picture them running around the large yard.

We had it painted a light tan to match the summer grasses that had waved in the July heat when we first saw the place. We started a large garden and grew much of our own vegetables, and I got to wander our hills like Johnny Appleseed, planting all manner of seedlings that would forever enrich our soil.

As our monetary wealth grew, so did my thoughts of taking things a bit more easily. I had been working nonstop at my practice for nearly ten years by that time, and my mind would often wander to the schedule I had held at Yosemite in my youth. It had been most relaxing, having that reprieve playing its part to ease the tensions and doldrums of constant hard work. Could I instill this into my own practice? Could I be taking things more easily? It *was*, after all, *my* practice. I could do as I wished.

I spoke with my secretary, and she seemed perfectly fine with the idea. She told me that she could use that week for cleanup and making headway on the backlog of paperwork that she constantly fought. When it came down to it, it was pretty easy to do. We simply stopped scheduling patients for the last week of every month.

During that week, if need be, I could always refer a patient to a friend or colleague, should any of them have emergency medical needs. I began telling new patients that this was the way that I operated, or *did not* operate, and I never heard one negative word about it. Instead, most people were envious of my schedule.

This great decision kick-started my life as a philosopher-surgeon and wandering poet. My family would join me in my fun when their lives allowed, but for the most part, it was just me and the land. Every fourth week, I would whisk myself away to whatever destination struck my fancy that month.

I spent four days wandering down the Amazon riding a river boat. I visited Niagara Falls. I fished for huge trout in remote parts of Alaska, and I rode the rapids of the Colorado River. I saw bald eagles feed their young, and I skydived into my beloved Yosemite National Park. I had found a balance that best suited me and my family. I worked hard and I played hard.

Years passed quickly with all of my adventures, both at home and away. Soon the kids were graduating, and headed off to college to start their own lives. Ellen and I found ourselves in our prime, with no children to worry about, and she became my full-time adventuring partner.

Having someone else along cuts much of the work out of travel, and it spreads out the responsibility. My wife was a champ in this area. She took over all the paperwork, booking necessities, food prep, packing, and so on.

This lightened my mental load a great deal, and it left me a lot more time to ponder and "philo-see-phize," as Ellen called it. She said that it made her laugh to say it like that, but I think it was her way of dealing with my necessary time away. Like she needed to separate my needs, as childish thoughts, to be kept away from those of Plato and Socrates and the like. But she dealt with it, like she always did.

I myself was better able to hone my own views of the world and the necessity of balancing one's societal life with meditation and reflection became apparent. I had, for the most part, lived in this manner my entire life without realizing it. This was my natural stasis, my individual frequency.

I was able to pass on my personal balance to my wife and children. Hopefully, they will do the same with their own children. I hope they will discover the great importance of finding one's own connection to the Earth. The necessity of natural play and creating happiness, along with ample time for introspective reflection. Offering kindness and respect for all beings. Giving to those in need, and loving with all that you are. When this balance is found, everything else in life falls into line.

Over the years, I witnessed some of the greatest achievements mankind had to offer. I watched men walk on the moon, and I witnessed the first supersonic flight. I saw the first computer taking up an entire office building, and I personally lived the great American Dream.

Progress on racial equality had been made consistently throughout my life, and greater change was coming about as a result of Tiffany's Law. The law removed all symbols of bigotry and hate from the country, labeled all who promote racism as social-terrorists, and furthered from the top down a clear message that racism will no longer stand in a country that is truly for *all* people. Once we removed the single religion influence from the government, and the men of the country no longer had a say in what happens to women's bodies, abortion was no longer considered an absolute evil, and was deemed necessary in some instances. The country was making progress where progress was sorely needed.

But we were far from perfect. Trickle-down economics does not work if the richest people in the world horde all the wealth. This policy left all classes other than those at the top struggling for survival and advancement. Energy was being wasted. Greed began to take hold, as it does in such cases, and it worked its way through the capitalistic society like a weed in the driveway. It clung to whatever crack it could find and it was always growing. America began placing its profits ahead of its citizens, and that begat its downfall, followed by the rest of the world.

*

I have reached the age of eighty-six, and I have now outlived my wife, who died from lung cancer, and one daughter who died by her own hand after battling depression and an abusive husband. My poor beautiful little girl even took her unborn child with her when she left us. Her husband now rots in some prison somewhere, very lucky that I was never able to get my hands on him…

I am now sitting on my California porch with a drink in my hand and watching my land burn. Climate change deniers, who grew in numbers with the election of the failed orange businessman, did not heed the warnings of scientists and the effects could not be reversed.

The president, whose bankruptcy track record continued with the entire nation when he thought that it would be OK to run the country like a business, ran this once mighty country into the ground. Religions did not police their own, and anyone with a Bible was given license to spew whatever nonsense they wanted as long as they could shoehorn it into the narrative. Armed fascists began terrorizing the country in the name of God.

There is no turning back for humanity now. We have damaged Earth far beyond repair. Even the Arctic is in flames… the fucking Arctic. Locust swarms have destroyed Australia, and the Covid plague wiped out ten percent of the Earth's population. The latter was furthered by our own president's utter refusal to set an example fit for "the greatest country" on Earth. His coziness with the Russians didn't last through his stay in power, and the entire world went into sharp decline after the relationship crumbled. It really does take a special person to change the world, and America's first dictator certainly fit at least one definition of "special."

My surviving daughter called me earlier this morning, saying that nuclear war was imminent. She had pleaded with me to go with her and her family to their fallout bunker they had put in years ago. She begged me, as the last member of her family, to go with them. I declined.

I have lived a great many places and have seen many things, but I don't think a bunker is for me. She begged me to come with them before the phone service cut out. But I am too old to be living in a box underground. My box will come soon enough.

So, here I sit in my paradise as the sirens begin to wail in the distance. Great hulking things, the sirens were, like the old air-raid warnings of the previous World Wars. They had been installed all across the country when it had become clear that peace would not be achieved and the nukes were placed back upon the table. These sirens announced the nuclear missiles.

The country has been all but destroyed. The dream, as well as the reality, was gone. It had been easy to crumble, as it turns out the country was nothing but a strawman. An economy based on pretend money that the government conjured with nothing tangible to back it up. They just printed more and more money to suit their needs.

Institutions that were actually *for* the people fell first, taking with them the stock market, and dragging the whole world's economy down with them. The great country began to turn on itself, in cannibalization, which left us vulnerable to attack.

Luckily, Ellen had passed away some years before all of this and she never even saw the beginning of the end. She would have been completely heartbroken by what our once proud country has become.

It wouldn't be long now. My old walking stick sat resting beside me, and I picked it up and rose from the table. I slowly walked down the wooden steps of the porch and headed along the trail to reach a higher elevation.

The small hill next to our house was still relatively untouched by the flames, and I made my way up there achingly, my body barely heeding my command these days. The hill offered me a three-hundred-and-sixty-degree look at the devastation. The fires were circling me. I could feel the heat; it looked like the house was just beginning to catch.

I heard my cup shatter on the porch. The winds shifted, and they took with them much of the obscuring smoke, allowing me to peer across the great valley where we had made our home. All I could see was ruin, and the bombs had not yet begun to fall.

*

There was no bolt of lightning, or any jolt of realization as I became aware. We were just all of a sudden whole again, with all of the knowledge of my mission and Us, fully intact.

I gazed down upon my withered octogenarian hands, and I took in this blaring change of routine. This man's daughter had been my mother. The one that was still here clinging to me along with Jacob. We were ALL connected, a string of lives moving towards some unknown purpose. I felt more whole.

It was a little weird. I had never joined with someone so advanced in age before. I could feel all the constant aches and pains that come with living for so long, but I could also feel his very being. I could feel the very depths of his soul. He had gotten it.

This man had deduced my message without any extra help from me. By simply living and reading the world around him, he had understood. A first of his kind. He understood that the inner working cogs of every entity all worked together to power only one thing, *the whole*. That treating everything and everyone with due respect was how the entire balance maintained itself. This man had gotten every bit of my message, and thankfully, he had taught his children.

But then I looked around at the smoldering devastation. The fucking dumbasses had really done it this time. The sirens were still calling out their impending doom. I had failed humanity forever. The events unfolding could wipe every human, animal, and plant from *the whole's* existence.

I mean, we always come back, one way or another. But it would take a long time for us to heal from the radiation. With humans gone, they wouldn't be able to fuck it all up with the furthering of their own harmful agendas. Newer, more productive life could find its own way.

The first missile hit the state capitol with an enormous boom that I felt deep in our old man chest, even over thirty miles away. The bombs had gotten much bigger since the last time I saw one explode.

The great mushroom of fire could be seen forming in the far-off sky, as we watched the next missile hit a bit further south. After that, it was one explosion after another, all along the spine of California, smiting the state out of existence and taking with it its vast population of "Libtards."

I was too far away to be hit by the actual nuclear blast. That would have killed me instantly, and it would have been easiest. But everything around Us would be covered in radiation soon, and *that* death was excruciating, I know.

Luckily, the grass fires were still burning the dry tinder on the small hill, and that would do just fine.

We sat down just like the time I had protested the Vietnam war: cross-legged, and holding a deep meditative pose. I prepared to burn.

It never came. I never felt the sting of the flames, and I never choked on the fiery air around me. The burning continued, but I just left. One moment we were there, ready to die, and the next, we were everywhere again. I had never been able to do this before. We left the enlightened man's body behind so that he might completely return to *the whole* and start fresh as soon as possible. I sent the old man's energy ahead of me to the pool and I turned to take in our entire being one last time.

Devastation was everywhere, and all that I could feel was sorrow. Huge piles of rubble were all we could see, and smoke and deadly radiation blanketed and choked the atmosphere. Life on Earth was dying. Someone had nuked the north pole, out of spite. In every country, in every state, and in every single corner of the world, pestilence and death rained down. The entirety of *the whole* had been razed.

I felt the urgency to go back to the pool with a pull stronger than ever before. It was yanking me back to our collective consciousness, and I was powerless to stop it. I got one last glimpse of the beautiful globe that was Us, and then I left the maddening carnage behind.

*

The pool was absolutely brimming with life, but not in a good way. The entire place felt like it was going to explode.

The nukes had sent most of the animals and plants from *the whole* back into the pool all at once, and big rivers of unexpected energy were still flowing in, tipping the balance precariously.

Ocean life would soon follow as the radiation slowly poisoned the seas. I didn't know how much the energy pool could hold, or if there even *was* a limit. Furthermore, it wasn't just good energy that came into the pool.

All around me, the negative energy fought with *the whole's* positive energy. The battle swelled, pulsating with conflict, and deep ripples of torment raged throughout the pool.

This was *our* struggle I was witnessing. The eternal struggle. It was the battle for the ages, the one that bards croon about. Good versus evil, the *final* showdown. What had ended all life as we knew it on *the whole* was now here in the pool, strengthening its void of brethren, threatening to destroy us for good.

The deep-seated negativity that so many humans had fostered and grown within themselves had been unleashed. It melded into a single pointed force of destruction. Its pent-up fury was more than enough to overpower the positive energy, and I watched in horror as the darkness rapidly began to consume the light.

I was helpless against the assault. It was like I was being torn in every direction at once, and I could feel my very essence diminishing into nothingness. Time slowed to a halt. The dark energy was barely being held at bay by the constant flow of positive energy that continued to stream into the pool. I knew this could not last, and I knew that we could not hold on to ourselves for much longer. I had to do something, but weakened as I was, and with my rapidly fleeting knowledge, I had no idea what.

A long tendril of darkness reached out for me. It sensed my indecision. I watched it void the world around itself as it moved back and forth, dancing. It tested our strength and resolve in order to judge its final assault.

It knew I was weak, and with a great calculated thrust, it parted the light's defenses and reached itself deep into me.

The darkness curled around my very essence and squeezed, begging me to join it. I could feel its devastation as it tore at the very fabric of *the whole's* being. Its forces of anger and hate began pulling Us apart atom by atom. The darkness commanded our death. It would be easy to let it all go and give in. Rest could finally be had after eons of soul-wrenching work. No more endless struggle, no more sadness, no more constant heartache as humanity rends themselves into oblivion.

It says that there are tacos…

I could stop this mission of mine and let *the whole* maintain itself. I could finally be fully at peace! I could just float away into the darkness. I could give in…

It was Mom who pulled me from evil's trance, as the void had all but lulled me away with its siren promises of tacos and peace of mind. But with the one final bits of herself, Mom managed to love one more time.

With a last pulse inside me, Mom exuded a final and eternal embrace, and was snuffed out of existence by the darkness.

It was this final act that brought me back. I knew my mission. It is, after all, what I *am*. Nothing was going to stop Us now. I took that last scrap of sacrificial love that was Mom, and I placed everything I ever was into it. Through her example, my actions became clear. I hugged it…

I reached out with all that we were, all that we had ever been, and I hugged the void. We could feel the darkness's shock at the act of kindness, and I started calling all of our energy back to me. I leaned into the embrace and focused all of our being into commanding every other part of the pool to "be like me."

I exuded my examples of compassion and love. Of kindness and generosity. I tightened my grip on the darkness and held it with all of my might. This. Is. How. To. Be!

With every particle of myself, every strand of DNA, and with everything I could ever possibly be, I pushed my message.

Nothing. I continued with the complete force of what remained of *the whole*, our very being stretched to its vast limits.

I remembered the Alamo.

Slowly, our efforts started to take hold. One tiny little bit of darkness in the middle of the rest up and decided to switch teams. Its void suddenly exploded with the spectrum of its decision, and that was all it took. The darkness's natural state was the light, so it was instinct to return.

Another followed, then another, and the transformation picked up more and more speed as the darkness realized the better way to be. It was returning to us. We didn't release our grip.

Quicker and quicker as we kept the pressure on, and then the change began to unfold all by itself. We did not have to push the darkness any longer. With a proper example of how to be, and how to conduct itself, the darkness was eager to change.

Our light became more powerful as we welcomed back those of us who had strayed so far. The energy filled us, and with a blink, we were again whole, as one.

Our pool was aglow with the happiness and joy of unity, long awaited.

*

Our metaphysical being would take some time as our terrestrial form mended. As soon as it had been wiped clean, small slivers of energy had already begun to flow back into our Earth, planting the seeds of life anew. The strong radiation repelled most of this, of course, but as the harmful energy would disperse over time, more and more light could enter and start the major regrowth that was needed.

We waited and bathed in our pool of newfound freedom for when we could return and ensure the removal of the blight from the land.

Chapter 7

I had to get up quietly so as not to awaken my little sister as she slept next to me. Maggie could not speak. She couldn't utter one word; she'd been born without vocal cords. She always loved it when I read to her before bed; she loved hearing my voice. She could read on her own, and I taught her how to write, and she could most certainly hear, so I had to deploy stealth mode.

Today was *her* day, and I was going to let her sleep in as long as possible. I quietly bent down and started to put on my shoes. In reaching to do so, I noticed that last night's candle had dripped its sticky blue wax everywhere. Maggie and I had both fallen asleep with our new book, and we had accidently left the candle to burn itself out. Wax had covered the novel that had fallen from my hands.

I picked the book up and tried my best to unstick some of the pages, but the wax had soaked through the paper and the pages ripped. Our new novel was a lost cause. We may never know what would become of the sordid romance between the vicar and the lonely heiress. C'est la vie. I would try to find another book while I was out searching today, and we can always make more candles, but I sure hated to miss an ending.

I slowly made my way through the clusters of people still asleep, tiptoeing as softly as I could around the scattered bedrolls that lay here and there throughout the cave. We had only recently found this natural shelter, but it seemed as if it could suit us for some time. Maybe we could finally put an end to the wandering.

There was a small bit of water running in the back of the cave, right down a sharp channel in the rock. The water seemed to be radiation free, but we could never really be sure about a new water supply until the babies started being born with more or fewer "limitations" than before. Regardless of the water conditions, the cave was definitely better than sleeping out in the open, or amid the teetering building rubble. If attacked, we could defend ourselves pretty well from this cave's vantage points. We needed to have a group discussion about it.

It was Maggie's sixth birthday. We knew this from the science books we'd had in the bunker with us, and had read over and over again throughout the years. The books had taught us that a year was 365¼ calendar days, so we kept marks on the small piece of wood that I always carried in my bag. I pulled the wood out of my knapsack, unsheathed my knife, and slashed her little birthday mark: day 113, April 23, 2035.

It had been just over ten years since the great nuclear world war that had almost wiped out the entire planet. Those that had shelters survived, and those that didn't were melted over time by the extreme radiation that ravaged the world. It had only been three years since our parents had been killed during the flooding of our fallout shelter. Apparently, nobody had thought about that danger. Our parents were the only family we had, except possibly for a grandpa out there somewhere. I could still remember the frantic phone call Mom had made to her dad, begging him to come be with us in the shelter. He had refused, choosing to meet his fate in his own way instead. We never found out what happened to him.

With our parents gone and our home underwater, there was nothing else to do. Maggie and I set off, not knowing if we would die from exposure or not. We were all alone for a while, just Maggie and me, and we got along fine walking. We ate whatever we were able to find. We slept in old houses and barns, and we stayed away from the main roads. We had one another and we were alive; that was all that really mattered.

Even though we loved each other, it was lonely, and we had to hide from anyone else we came across. There were gangs out there who didn't care about others. They would kill most everyone. Though because we were children, we would most likely have become their slaves.

A wandering group found us one day when my sister got her foot stuck in the floorboards of an old house we had been scavenging. Maggie didn't yell, of course, but the crash of the boards was enough to alert the group. Luckily for us, they weren't pirates or murderers, and they didn't skin or chain us. What they did was help me get poor Maggie's foot unstuck.

There were about thirty of them in total. A motley assorted crew of raggedly dressed men, women, and children, all with some limitation or another (growths, mostly) and one really old guy with a beard who was their Leader. It was Leader's teaching that led to the group's belief that the Earth could only heal through complete unity. But the group also carried guns in case of danger.

This group of people chose not to rob, cheat, or kill in order to maintain their meager existence. They believed in being tolerant and open-minded to another's point of view, but that the intolerance of others was gravely intolerable. They offered a path of love and kindness through their unity.

Their beliefs rung true with little Maggie, as she sat there and listened to the group talk about themselves and their mission. She began to pull on my sleeve and nodded along with them as we listened. She looked up at me with pleading eyes, and I understood. Maggie needed to go with them. That was the only thing she had ever asked me for. So, even though I was still a bit skeptical, we joined the small group of wanderers on their journey west.

The forest was barely returning around the foothills that housed the cave. Plant growth was sporadic due to the radiation fallout, but here it was growing slowly, nonetheless. Small redwood shoots had started their skyward journeys, the strongest of their kind that had survived the blasts. Grasses were coming back, and their small blades were long enough to dance slightly with the breeze. Strangely shaped bushes grew everywhere, with clusters of long gnarled branches growing with no rhyme or reason. They had long thorns that tugged at my clothing as I passed, and I felt one snap as my pant leg grazed a bit too closely. They were brittle; life still struggled. But some tiny birds had begun darting about in the bush undergrowth at the sound of the breaking twig, and it was good to see healthy animals again.

It was harder for me than most of the others. My limitation was an increasingly crooked back. It could be worse, and it will be eventually, but walking put a strain on my spine that led to a constant ache. I was used to it and have developed a gait that doesn't hurt terribly badly, but it often left me far behind the group. This was why I liked exploring places alone. I could walk at my own pace and meander as I saw fit.

I headed further west for a bit, because we had just come in from the east. I traveled for about an hour through the waving grasses. I had to stop for a rest on a rock. I looked towards the morning sun, and saw a farmhouse in the distance that I had passed by. Well, shoot. I could push on further to see what I could find, and then take a look at this place when I headed home to the cave. I shifted on the rock and I felt the ache in my back, and I decided that I had already come too far. I slid off of the rock and headed towards the old homestead.

The farmhouse was dilapidated, and it had clearly already been ransacked from the looks of mess everywhere. But it had made it out of the fires unscathed, so it had some possibility. I picked my way through the overgrowth to the house. The paint was nearly gone, though I could see flakes of white and green that still clung to the window frames. The front door lay broken and hanging from the one remaining bottom hinge, and offered no obstruction, even for someone with a crooked back. There were dusty pictures still hanging on the wall. I brushed one off, then another, and another as I moved towards the back of the house.

The family who had lived here had been on this farm for a few generations, and their story was evident through their photographs as I moved down the hallway. Great-grandchildren, grandkids, kids, all playing around the vast property. There was a boy on a small green tractor sitting next to his dad who rode a real tractor. Someone playing fetch with the family dog. A tree house in the backyard. Life was *so* incredibly different now.

One picture had fallen to the floor, and I picked it up. Brushing the coating of dust off revealed an old farmer and his wife. Presumably the owner of this farm, and the patriarch of this family. They reminded me of my own grandparents and their property in what used to be called California. Mom's parents had owned a hundred acres of pastoral land, and I remembered running through the long grass as a child. After Grandma died from cancer, our family ended up moving one state over. It was there that Dad built the bunker, and it was there that Grandpa refused to join us. There was more than one time after our parents died that I had wished for Grandpa's jokes and know-how. I missed him...

I hung the picture back up on its hook and went all the way into the back of the house to begin my sweep of the rooms for any useful items that might still be around. Most of the clothing had already been taken, but in the pocket of a crumbling old rain jacket I found a new Bic lighter that still worked; those always came in handy. In another room, under a dilapidated desk, I found a few wrinkled pages of a magazine about old movies and the actresses and actors who starred in them, and I folded those away for later; the kids would like those. I found a few hot sauce packets underneath an old cushion leaking foam, and I found a bent fork I could fashion into a spearhead for fishing. I came to the stairs and moved carefully so they wouldn't collapse and take me down with them.

They creaked and groaned under my weight, but I hugged the wall as I went, and I made it all the way up without falling. The second story was a bit cleaner except for the dust. The flood waters hadn't reached this high so except for the looting, it was all relatively intact. There were a few bed frames that still held tattered mattress remnants. Dressers with their drawers strewn about stood whole against the walls.

In the bathroom, the bathtub held a stinky nest of some sort. Possibly a racoon by the size of it and the black and gray tufts of fur, but the nest seemed to have been long abandoned. The sink above the mirror was shattered, spiderwebs of cracks running all the way to the edges. I looked at myself in the mirror fragments and waved at myself before leaving the room.

As I was coming out of the bathroom, a strange breeze hit me from directly above. I looked up to see the attic access hanging slightly ajar. The pull cord had long since wasted away, so I jumped in order to catch the door's lip, my fingers only just grasping it. It was possible that the previous scavengers had missed looking up here. I crossed my fingers and hoped.

The ladder swung down with a loud squeak, followed by a thud as it hit the floor. I instinctively looked out of the windows for anyone who might be around to hear the noise. When I heard nothing, I climbed up the old ladder to see what awaited me there.

It was dark and musty in the attic and smelled like mold. The window glass had not been shattered up here, so nature had not been able to take over. The dust covered everything that wasn't sticky with cobwebs, from the rafters to the floor, and my feet left deep impressions in the grime as I searched around.

The lack of direct light played tricks with the shadows, and my eyes had to get used to the difference. There didn't seem to be anything there; the whole attic appeared bare. My heart sank, I had gotten my hopes up. Maybe there was something in the barn I could give to Maggie. But as I turned to leave, a gust picked up outside and blew through the leaves on the tree in front of the window.

More light streamed, and there in the corner, I spied what looked like a dust-covered sheet. It too was covered in the deep layer of grime, and the form almost completely blended in with its surroundings. From the way it was shaped, it had to be protecting something.

The roof pitch forced me to stoop painfully as I moved closer, and soon I gave up and began to crawl. The lump wasn't all that big, maybe two by three feet, and about two feet tall.

I poked it. There was something solid under the cover. I sat beside it and turned my head away to avoid the dust before whipping the sheet back.

It was an old trunk. Still in very good condition. The etched leather handles were only just beginning to show signs of decay. It was roughly rectangular in shape, except for an arching lid with a large clasp, and it featured metal reinforcements that helped to keep it rigid. It was covered with stickers, each representing a faraway place. "Paris," "Thailand," "The Big Apple!" (That one sounded interesting; Maggie had only seen pictures of apples, and I would like to see the big one.) The trunk was still locked, and the clasp wouldn't budge when I tried it. I removed the pocketknife my dad had given me when I was seven from my pocket, and with a few jiggles of the blade, the clasp sprung open with a pop. The lid lifted up an inch or two, and the smell that came from inside the trunk was… human.

Not like a dead body, quite the opposite actually; it smelled of human life, or human life before the war. Mixed in with the scent of cedar in the box was the rich smell of fresh clothes and laundry detergent. Mom had used to wash all of our clothes in a machine during the first few years of bunker life. Even when we lost all power, we still washed our clothes weekly in a big tub, but eventually we ran out of detergent. I will always remember that particular smell; it reminded me of my parents.

The top of the trunk was filled with an assortment of clothes. There were a few old T-shirts that looked like they had just been thrown in, but they looked like they would fit me. I picked up the top one and held it up. "Richmond Family Reunion '95." I stuck the shirt into the bottom of my sack.

Underneath the shirts was a tiny dress. It had been carefully folded and preserved in a plastic bag draped from a small hanger. It was light pink and covered in delicate white lacy frills that were most likely hand stitched by a loving family member. It had a small silver brooch pinned to it just under the neckline. The trinket was roughly disk shaped, but scalloped around the edges. There was a large tree etched into it, but its branches were like ropes that wove in and out of each other endlessly. I had never seen anything quite like it, so I unpinned it and stuck it in my pocket. The dress was much too small for Maggie (who was already a fraction of what she should be for her age) so it had to have been for a baby. I put the dress in my sack on top of the T-shirt, laying it carefully as to not crease it.

Underneath the dress was a leather photo album, which I didn't look at, but moved to the side out of my way. There wasn't likely to be anything of use in it, and I could always look later. Below the album was a fluffy white wedding dress. This too was wrapped in a plastic sheeting, and it took up the rest of the trunk. Such a garment was virtually useless these days, as nobody could function in it. It would be completely torn to shreds by the underbrush, should anyone attempt to wear it and walk around.

I put it with the album and started to wonder if I would be able to lug the empty chest all the way back to the cave by myself. Maggie would certainly love it as a birthday present, and I could make wheels for it if we decided to keep moving. I lifted the trunk by the handles to test its weight and I felt something heavy shift in the box. I ran my fingers around the bottom and caught a glimpse of a small hole in the corner.

I set the box back down and again took out my knife. I stuck it in the hole and worked the blade around the edge a bit. Soon, the whole false bottom popped out to reveal a secret compartment. Whatever was in there was wrapped in a woman's large handkerchief with an embroidered floral pattern that was made up of light blue daisies upon a sea of off-white.

This would be the perfect present for my sister, although white things do not stay very white anymore. I had a beautiful gift, regardless of whatever else was in the trunk.

I slowly removed the wrapping and tucked it away gently in my pocket. There, in the bottom of the old trunk, lay a pristine family Bible.

The golden inlaid lettering shone brightly as I turned it over in my hands, and I instinctively held the tome up to my nose in order to capture its unique leather scent. Many of the Leader's group-lessons had come from this ancient book. (Well, from the New Testament and Jesus's direct teachings.) I had personally seen pieces of Bibles over the past years, and I read as much as I could when I was given the opportunity, but I had never seen one in its entirety. This could be the very last Bible in the whole world.

I was awestruck. Everything one is supposed to need was written in this book. With this, we could begin to rebuild society as it once was. I overcame my shock, and I hurriedly dumped the wedding dress out of its hanging cover. I carefully wrapped the Bible in the plastic, making sure to tie each of the ends together, should I encounter rain on my way back to the cave. Once it was packaged, I carefully padded it along the sides with the T-shirts, in case I bumped into anything, and firmly secured the Bible in my bag.

I had more than I had come for – more than I ever could have hoped for – and I made my way back over to the ladder. I stepped carefully down the creaking ladder and landed safely on the second floor with my new prizes. I started to head down the stairs to the first floor, but turned back to the attic entrance after a moment.

I went back, folded the ladder up, and used an old piece of railing to push the hatch back up into place. The secret attic would remain a secret and I still might come back to get the trunk. My back was sore from sitting under the eave and I really wanted to get back to the group to share my treasure, so I gingerly navigated my way down the staircase, and I headed towards "home."

Even though my back was killing me from the walking, I made it back to the cave much quicker than I anticipated. I felt rejuvenated by my incredible find, and I could feel its words calling out for me from my satchel to read them. Its calls gave me the energy to push through my back pain, and I was back at the base of the cave before I knew it. The whole ordeal had only taken about four hours, and I felt accomplishment like I hadn't experienced in some time.

Maggie ran up to hug me as I crested the rim of the cave. She always hated it when I left the group before she was awake, and she looked a little teary. But I leaned down and whispered "just you wait, Little Missy" into her ear, and she smiled up at me quizzically.

"Nope, I'm not showing you anything yet. Even birthday girls need to be patient." My eyes shone with delight and a bigger smile crept across her face. She hadn't even remembered that it was her birthday.

I motioned for her to sit and wait and I shuffled painfully to our spot to set down the very heavy bag. I stretched and groaned. I might have overdone it for the day, and I was extremely glad that I had decided not to bring the trunk back as well.

The group began to gather around Maggie and me as I slumped down onto my bedroll, and I leaned my back against the cold cave wall. I could smell food cooking and my stomach gave a gurgling lurch, but it would have to wait. The group could feel that something big was happening, and they crowded in closer. I began to open my bag, but then remembered, and I reached into my pocket and pulled out the magazine bits.

I handed them to some of the children, who ran off to see what they contained. I removed the tiny dress from the bag and gave it to an expectant mother, whose eyes lit up as she told me that her baby will be a girl who could wear it. As she ran off to stash the dress, I could see the glint of the brooch in the firelight. Leader spoke up and said, "It was called a baptism dress. To be worn when a baby was given a name as they bathed in the waters of God."

I thanked him for the details, before I announced to the group that it was Maggie's birthday and that she was six years old. I told the others about how our parents would be very proud of her for all she had gone through, and that if they could be here with us today, they would have made sure she got a grand present for being the very special little girl that she was.

I looked down at my sister sitting in the dirt next to me, and saw her eyes well with tears at the mention of our parents. I removed the new handkerchief from my pocket, and she could no longer hold in her emotional onslaught. She grabbed the handkerchief and sobbed into it. I pulled her close to me and held her like I've done ever since she was a baby. Like all big brothers do when their little sisters need them. After a few minutes, after Maggie's great sobs were reduced to a light shake of her shoulders, I reached over and removed the big plastic package from my bag.

I handed the book over to Leader, and he raised his eyebrows as I said, "I have found what we've been looking for... Even if we didn't know we were looking for it."

Leader walked to a spot by the fire so that he could see better in the light. He sat down on a rock and placed the package on his lap. He slowly undid my carefully tied knots and began unwinding the book's plastic wrap. He glanced back at me quickly, his questioning eyes widening as it became clear to him what he was holding. I grinned and nodded my assurance to the man. His hands were shaking as he took out the Bible. The golden letters shimmered in the dancing firelight, and a large gasp went through the group. Those who did not know what it was that Leader held looked around expectantly at those who did. But no one could take their eyes off of the Bible to acknowledge them. Leader stood up, a bit unsteadily, and looked around, addressing the entire group at once.

He tried to speak. He tried to pass on the great weight of our find, and tried to explain the importance of it, not just for our little group, but for all of humanity. He tried. I could see it all in his eyes, he tried. But he never got a word out.

Maggie leapt from my lap, crying no more. With a gurgling roar she should not have been able to make, she dashed towards the Leader. She reached up and snatched the Bible from his hands and began tearing out its pages, tossing them in the fire. The group watched in horror.

*

Once again, I was complete.

The Us had finally released me from my hiatus, and I was more full of life than ever before. I had never been in the energy pool for that long, and it had given me more purpose, an extra skip to my soulful step.

Young Maggie and I joined as her brother comforted her. No spasms or eye rolling, just a complete exchange of energy and knowledge.

Being held was nice. After the battle and my hibernation, and after being in the pool without a body for so long, I needed to feel another being. Not the inner energy feeling of the pool, but real, skin to skin, physical human touch.

The little girl's crying had stopped when we merged. Her sad thoughts of her parents and of happier times had been replaced by the knowledge of Mom and Dad being everywhere around her. We sat, held our brother, and enjoyed his love.

It was the gasp of the group that interrupted our family time. I looked up from my brother's arms to see what had caused such a reaction. That is when I saw that what the Leader had been holding was a Bible.

Every failed life that I had ever lived took control over little Maggie and me.

We grew enraged. All of my frustration and heartache, all of the death and destruction, all of the negative energy that had been allowed to flourish, brimmed inside of me until it threatened to spill over.

Time and time again, throughout all of history, humans have taken my message and corrupted it with their hubris and greed. Humans have bastardized my simple examples of compassion and humility, of honoring the whole, of servant leadership, and love for *all*, and have used them to create vast pyramid schemes of imbalance and tyranny. They provided humans with a means to push their *human* agendas onto others and to oppress those who dared think otherwise. They fed the darkness. Not that it was religion's fault, but the misuse of religion was the reason for the most heinous of atrocities.

Some king thinks he is equal to "God," and he doesn't happen to like homosexuals, so he assumes he is worthy of changing sacred text. Thus, thousands of years of unnecessary persecution for innocent gay people.

Like any omnipotent God of eternal love and understanding would create something only to have their creation shunned by everyone. That is not balance. Like any capable God would allow innocent children to die around the world, then condemn them to an eternal hell, just because they were born in a place where a certain Bible doesn't exist.

Women being second-class citizens! No mixing textiles! No working on Sunday! Stoning! It goes on and on. No shellfish, no eating ferrets, no short hair, *must* have a beard, no divorce, no jewelry, no period-sex, don't curse at your parents, etc. It was all absurd, and I had never said any of it.

Oh, and what fucking part of slavery, as it is so glorified in *the* text, is about loving thy neighbor or having compassion for others? Captivity has not a goddamn thing to do with love!

And last but not least, let us not forget that victims of rape are then supposed to marry their rapists…

It was too much. I couldn't bear it any longer. I would not let this chance at a new beginning be maligned by the same mistakes that had already led us to this desolate point in our history.

With a cry, I threw my new handkerchief down into the dirt, and with bared teeth of fury, I launched myself at Leader and snatched the Bible from him.

I heard screams of disbelief as I began ripping out great clumps of pages from the leather binding and throwing them into the fire.

The Old Testament first, as it was all fables and repurposed lore from older religions, further skewed to fit *human* narratives and desires. Even the Ten Commandments were fairly useless, should people follow my simple examples: The Beatitudes, for instance.

I tore at the Bible blindly.

Leader tried to stop me, he reached out to grab at the book, his face full of sadness. Even my astonished brother tried to help but I would not let either of them touch it.

I was a seasoned veteran now, the champion of *the whole*, the vanquisher of all things dark and evil. I would continue to fulfil my mission.

I pulsed. I used just enough of *the whole* around me, to "shimmer," all of the molecules in the air. The end result was a wave, like a pebble dropped into a creek. A concentrated ripple of *the whole* that sent both my brother and Leader reeling. I did not hurt them, I just pushed them away.

I could not say what it was that I was doing, or even who it was I had become, but they felt the great change that stood before them. The fire climbed high as I added more and more fuel. Page after page, through the entire book of misrepresentations.

"Damn it all!" I screamed in my head, tossing in the leather binding. We would start anew, with all of the teachings coming directly from my metaphysical mouth.

The flames leapt high behind me as the leather began to catch. The gold letters curled and pooled into drops that ran down the face of the cover and into the fire. I watched them with an air of completion and contempt, and I turned back to the little group.

Their faces were awash with a mixture of shock and fear, but the group knelt as I faced them. Slowly, each and every one of them lowered themselves before me.

"No," I whispered in my head. The placement of one being above another was everything I had been fighting against my entire existence. There would be no more subjugation in this world. There would be no more demand for respect, as those who have to demand are not worthy of respect in the first place. There would be no more kneeling before kings or Gods. There would be no more false prophets.

My being and these beings were no different. That is, except for my awareness of *the whole*.

I walked over to where my brother was sitting, his head bowed before me. I bent down and lifted his chin with my fingers until he raised his eyes to mine. I smiled at him, our special brother-sister smile, and I nodded for him to follow me.

I stood up and took his hand, pulling him from his penitent pose. We walked back to the hearth and I urged him in front of the fire beside me. I looked out at the firelit eyes of the group, firmly fixed upon us.

I turned to our brother, and then took each of his hands in mine. I looked up at him, gave him a wink and reassuring squeeze, and I passed to him all of my knowledge.

I watched in fascination as he jerked, and his eyes rolled back into his head, but a smile began to form on his lips and I knew that he would be fine. I had never seen someone else go through this transformation, and it was interesting to see something completely new. Now, *We* were aware.

One by one, each of them came to join hands with my brother and me, the entire group was passed the message of *Us*. Until finally, there we all stood, holding hands in an enlightened circle. A group of destitute humans, ravaged by radiation, in a cave aglow with flames fueled by dogma. We were the last known hope for *the whole*.

Beside me, my brother's hum took me by surprise as he began emitting a low F-sharp in the *Om*. This was something our dad had used to do when he was trying to get us to go to sleep at night. It was meant to focus us, and it did, but we never really knew exactly *what* it was.

We were all well aware of its exact power now. All around, *the whole* began to vibrate along with him, and I joined in.

There was a very good reason why people had chanted the *Om* for centuries. That single note, that one clear sound, was the absolute resonance of everything. Every plant, every animal, every rock. Every single particle knew this note. It was the mainstay of every other frequency. It was the head cornerstone of our very inner being.

The chant reverberated through the cave as the whole group picked it up. The cave itself started to hum. The sound connected the group to *the whole*, it made us one.

The chant grew as the soil beneath us joined in, its deep rumblings stemming from the very depths of nature itself. The strangely shaped bushes sang along and swayed precariously in their fragility, but complete Earthly unity was worth the risk.

The nearby redwood saplings caught on, and every single blade of grass vibrated in unison. They were part of us, and we were a part of them.

Through the connection, I showed everything how it would be. I drew upon the great rivers of energy that I called from the energy pool, and I gifted my example to all.

Our sphere of influence grew larger, our message compounded through the group and nature itself. We could feel our energy reaching far past our little cave.

It pushed and strained as we exuded our *good.* All around the cave, the meager plant life had burst into bloom. We could feel new life springing forth in concentric circles from where we stood.

We reached the ocean, some eighty miles away, and once our message was heeded by the Pacific, it quickly brought the other oceans with it.

We could feel us growing vast.

We washed over the abandoned cities and the fallen forests. We washed over the deepest valleys and we overtook the tallest peaks. We overran the gangs of marauders and peaceful survivors alike. We drew the radiation into us and then used its great power to do our bidding.

We used its own force to push our mission closer to completion. We felt ourselves reaching a wall, but we pushed harder and we drew upon each other and the world around us for support. And then, with a final little click, it was done. We had blanketed the entire *whole* with our knowledge and the message of love. My mission was finally complete.

*

We live an entirely peaceful life. *The whole* regrew and healed itself. The trees and plants returned to their full luster, but looked quite different than they used to. Surviving animals began their own new mutated paths of evolution.

The whole was free from mass pollution and dumping. Free from prejudices and free from hate. Free from bigotry and free of fear. Free from war and famine, plague and pestilence.

Free, completely free.

Every being understood how best to operate. Humans strive for goodness in all they do, exuding positivity, enriching their immediate environments and everything they touch.

Every single neutron, every single proton, every single electron, every single entity of *the whole* rings with songs of truth, balance, love, and kindness. Of equality and understanding.

Just as *God* intended.

Chapter 8

Tomorrow was the twenty-fifth day of the third month in the year. Renaissance Day. The anniversary of the Great Being unifying the world as one. Not only was the holiday most looked forward to, but this year was also the tricentennial anniversary of the great occasion and the celebration was going to be huge. Our village had been jittery with excitement for weeks while everyone prepared for the event, and my enthusiasm was no different. This year, I have finally hit teenager status and am now old enough to join the unification ceremony.

The morning sun's rays hit me precisely at their designated time, and I awoke feeling like a little kid again. I was excited for the celebration and the feasts that would take place tomorrow, but most importantly, I was excited to be part of the ceremony.

I remembered to set my alarm for earlier the next morning. I didn't want to miss the opening festivities, and I figured that waking up just after dawn would ensure me a good spot in the front.

I walked across my bedroom where the early morning light poured through. I closed my eyes and placed a hand under the small portal in the wall that allowed the sun to enter the room at any time, and I silently asked it to move. I opened my eyes again, and watched as the little window began to inch its way through the wood to the new position that would awaken me just before the sun rose the next morning.

I didn't have to specify exactly when, *the whole* knew what I wanted, and it responded to my needs. Everything now happens via the complete balance and connection we maintain with *the whole*.

Even my room itself was created out of my necessity. As a small child, I had stood and watched the village elders come together and focus their unified connection upon The Birth Tree. In response, the ground rumbled as hundreds of the tree's roots poked above ground and started to form saplings. The saplings grew and grew, reaching for the sky, widening as they went. They began to touch each other, and soon they became a single rising wall that attached itself to the southern side of The Tree. The rumbling grew more intense, and I remembered feeling my little feet growing numb from the vibration. I couldn't see what was taking place on the inside, but the huge tree-fingers continued upward in their journey to catch up to their surrounding brethren. I could hear the creaking and groaning of The Tree as it morphed to accommodate its new addition. When it was over, and after the elders had retired to have a cup of tea, I wandered inside what was to be my new home.

At that age, the room seemed enormous to me. I cried at the thought of living in such a big place all by myself. I looked around at what the room held. The Tree had been asked to grow itself to suit my needs. Inside, the grains of wood had grown into a roof about ten feet high, and there were three round windows aside from the small waking one.

A bed had grown to my perfect dimensions (it would adjust for my increasing body size) and it was topped with a soft green moss that cradled me while I dreamed. A small breakfast nook sat under one of the windows, and a wall of knots and whorls hid my bathroom facilities. The water for the shower and toilet was pumped up from deep within the ground, and any waste was directly returned to *the whole* to be utilized where it was useful.

Small-windowed spheres of bioluminescence appeared along the walls to provide more light when needed. Some even glowed in the closet from which I grabbed my clothes.

I remembered the lore of The Birth Tree as I chose a particularly festive-looking shirt. This very tree that I lived in, The Birth Tree, was said to be the final resting place of the original Being of knowledge and love. It was this Being that had for millions of years tried to keep the balance of *the whole* intact. Life after life, it pleaded with them to hear its messages.

For thousands of years, *the whole* had struggled uncontrollably, and ultimately became locked into a downward spiral of greed and fear. Humanity did not listen to The Being's many attempts at providing the better way, and they destroyed most of themselves, and much of *the whole* in the end.

The Being alone faced a raging army of pure evil. It was able to summon all of its strength and rally the remaining good energy in unification to evil's utter defeat.

In celebration of the win, The Being gave its knowledge of *the whole* to the Chosen Thirty, and they in turn started humanity's new life. The Being, having finally accomplished its mission, was said to have retired to spend its days living among the trees. This room I was dressing in – my home – was said to be The Being's heart, housing its very essence.

I wandered out after I finished getting dressed. Down the natural hallway and through the recesses of The Tree until I found myself in what we call the kitchen. This room was filled with natural light, though it still had little lamps hanging from the walls for nighttime use. The huge windows accommodated the morning sun and allowed it to spread its rejuvenating rays to the flora that resided within.

Here, joined through *the whole* to The Birth Tree, were all manner of fruits, nuts, and fungi, bits of dried protein and edible flowers of all different shades, all of it to be eaten. Bananas and coconuts hung from the ceiling, vines of mixed berries clung to the walls, and clusters of grapes grew out of every quaint little table scattered throughout the room. Once picked, the plants would immediately regrow in a never-ending buffet of human sustenance.

I was the only one who used the kitchen every day, being the only person who actually lived here, so I considered it mine. Because of this, I was surprised when I walked in to find my friend Aaron sitting in his painting clothes at one of the tables.

He must have been up early trying to "capture the sun's birth" again, as he put it, with his paints. His speckled multihued hands were busy cutting up a mango. He sensed me coming, and smiled as I reached up and chose a dragon fruit for myself. Aaron started talking hurriedly as I sat down across from him.

"Guess what I heard Atty?" he asked me, using my nickname, short for Atticus, and before I could answer, he continued, "You'll never be able to guess! OK, I got up before it was light out and I climbed up one of the pine trees out by the pond. You know the big one that has that crooked part about halfway up?" I nodded, my mouth full of fruit.

"Well, I wanted to get the sunlight bouncing off the pond, you know? I was sitting up there in the tree and starting to sketch out my painting," he said as he pointed to his small new canvas that sat on the mossy floor alongside his backpack. ""Two of the elders walked underneath me. They stopped by my tree as one of them picked a rock from his sandal and they were talking about Renaissance Day tomorrow. I was trying to ignore them and work on my sketch, but then I heard exactly what they were saying!" With this, he rose from his seat and started dancing around the room.

"Do you know what they said? DO YOU?" Aaron grew more excited as he recounted his morning adventure. He began jumping around the room. "They said that the remaining See'r, the last surviving member of the Thirty, was going to come here, to our village for Renaissance Day!"

I spit out my fruit as Aaron yanked me out of my seat and began twirling me in a waltz around the kitchen. It took me a moment to realize the meaning of these words, and I was soon joining in with Aaron's dancing hijinks.

The Thirty had gone on from their initial enlightenment to spread out across *the whole*. Their presence in the world ensured that a physical manifestation of *the* knowledge was ever present and ever vigilant among the human aspects of our entirety. There could be no return to the old ways of disconnection with the chosen keeping watch. Having been touched by The Being itself, the Thirty had lived on for generations, diligently keeping intact that which once had been so very broken.

They started to pass away eventually. Over the past hundred years or so, one by one, the village would receive the knowledge of their deaths through *the whole*. When this happened, the entire world would stop all its progress and spend days mourning these prophets of compassion.

Now there was only the one left. Her human name was Maggie, and she was turning three hundred and six years old the day of the holiday. She had been born mute in the midst of a greatly changing world, and she was the first host when the great purge of evil took place. She was the only person alive that knew both the old *and* the new way of life. No one surpassed her in fame, and she was coming here.

"Wait..." my mind said. "Maggie the *See'r* was coming here, to where I live... Oh no!"

My joy stopped immediately and I let go of Aaron as he continued to bound around the room until he saw me slumped down in the chair.

"What's going on? What happened? This is exciting!" Aaron said as he sat back down, out of breath.

I didn't know what to say. I certainly couldn't tell him the truth, and I searched my brain to come up with a valid excuse for why I wasn't happy. I poked at my fruit for a second before answering.

"It's just going to be so much more work now," I said. "I haven't even finished the preparations I was supposed to do already, and now I'm sure there will be tons more." I threw this at him, hoping that the flimsy excuse would stick.

"Bah, you've never scoffed at some extra work before, why now?" he asked. "And dude, it's the SEE'R!" He punched me on the arm and I used it to my advantage. I began grabbing at him like we were about to start a wrestling match right there in the kitchen.

He dodged my half-hearted attempts, but I was able to distract him from his skepticism about my change in mood. "I guess you're right," I said. "I'm just behind again, and I didn't sleep so well last night," I lied.

"Have you been in the elder's stash of special mushrooms again," he asked as he pulled me in for a headlock. "We all sleep like babies every night; *the whole* allows us total peace," he told me as I wiggled out of his grip. I didn't have a response, so instead, I pushed him over into the strawberry patch and ran.

He chased me as I knew he would. Aaron was always a bit faster than me, so I also knew that he would catch me soon. But I had a head start, and was off into the forest before he could get back up. I heard him calling out behind me.

"Ooooo, you're going to get it! I'm going to throw you in the pond, Atty!" We laughed as we ran, and I darted in and out of the trees to avoid his grasp.

"OK, OK! I give up!" I finally told him, my arms raised in submission. I came out from behind the large redwood that protected me. Aaron grabbed me in a hug. I squeezed him back, and I smiled as we walked back to get Aaron's bag from the kitchen. My secret was still safe.

*

Secrets do not tend to remain hidden for long in small villages. Big ones like a visit from the last See'r spread like seeds in the wind. The morning laziness was gone as Aaron and I walked back and we could hear the hubbub long before we even got close.

"Everyone will know by now," he said. I agreed as I reached up and brushed some squashed strawberry from his hair.

We got to the kitchen and Aaron grabbed his stuff. We walked back through The Tree and went out the front. The "face" of The Birth Tree looked over the village square. It was there that the people gathered any time momentous news was announced.

After the great war, *the whole's* human population had been decimated. Humans were now a tiny fraction of what they once were, and villages only held around two hundred people each. Every single member of our village stood in front of The Birth Tree. They were gathered in small groups of family and friends, and they all spoke quickly to each other in hushed tones.

Aaron and I sat down on the root-bench that stood off to the side of The Tree. We watched as the talk ceased and the groups began to part in order to provide room for the single-file line of the elders who made their way to the middle of the square.

The most senior elder was helped by his peers up onto the large and flat speaking rock that had been put there for this purpose and he shuffled slowly up to it to address the crowd.

"People of the Tree!" He spoke out in a voice that boomed over the heads of the gathered. "By now I am sure you have all heard the rumor, otherwise you would not be here. We, the elders, have come to tell you that the rumor is true. Maggie, the last See'r, will indeed be here at The Birth Tree for the celebration of the Renaissance. She is to be here by the day's end."

The roar of jubilation in response was so great that I could feel it in my chest. Aaron jumped up beside me and joined the group, clapping and hooting with teenage joy. He laughed and tried to pull me up with him, but he gave up when I refused to play along and he retreated back to the others in celebration.

I couldn't move. I couldn't be happy. I sat there on the bench and watched the entire village dance along to a beat that was unknown to me. The Birth Tree behind me even started to sway along with their happiness as they unified as one in their shared emotion. I realized I was out of character, and knew that I had to remain hidden for as long as possible.

I overcame my shock at the news and jumped up to join Aaron. I added my own clapping along with the beat and he hugged me and ruffled my hair as the elder held up his arms for silence.

The group quieted and the elder began to speak again. "We have indeed been blessed on this holiday celebrating the great evolution of humanity. Maggie will return to her place of birth and provide for us a unity ceremony that will rival the original." A cheer broke out again and the elder had to quiet the crowd once more.

"Some of us will need to head over to the Sacred Cave and make it more accommodating for the See'r. She has insisted on sleeping in her old home."

Aaron shot me a glance but didn't wait for a sign of agreement before he raised both our hands to volunteer. I started to protest, but then realized this would get me out of my normal duties and away from all of the extra preparations around the village, so I went along with it and nodded along with Aaron as the elder pointed to us. "OK, Atty and Aaron will take care of the cave, the rest of you stick around for further instructions."

The elder clapped twice, and the two of us ran off to change and pack our bags with things we would need for our hike. Aaron followed me to my room and sat on the bed as I went to the closet to get my backpack. I grabbed a different shirt and changed out of the fancy one I'd worn to the party. I didn't want it to get stained and the rocks of the cave were sharp enough to snag the embroidered flowers that wound around the neck and wrists. The shirt I chose instead was dyed a dark brown and was made from strong hemp. It was a work shirt, and I pulled it over my head as Aaron started talking.

"We can stop by my house on the way out of the village. My mum was just putting in some loaves of bread when I left this morning; we can take one with us. I haven't been to the caves in years. When was the last time you were there?" he asked as I adjusted the shirt.

"I don't know," I told him. "It was with my parents... Before the accident."

Aaron grew quiet and he began to rub his knee uncomfortably. "It's OK, dude," I added. "I know they're both all around me in everything I do and see. We all return to the pool one way or another, it was just their time."

"I know, and I feel them around you constantly," Aaron told me, then confessed, "but I also know that you get into your moods where you don't want to talk, and I don't want you being quiet our entire trip to the cave." He smiled, and I smiled back.

"Come on, you big goof," I told him as I punched him in the arm. "Let's go get that bread." We ran through the polished wooden hallways and out the back door.

We stopped running when we reached the path that ran along behind The Tree. We slowed down to take our time along the winding way through the forest. I could see Aaron up ahead of me taking in the natural wonder surrounding our village. I looked around us as we walked and enjoyed the singing birds and fields of waving flowers we passed, but from how others had explained it to me, I didn't *feel* right.

Yes, *the whole* responded to my needs, but I didn't feel like I could join in unity as the others did. I had to ask *the whole* for what I needed while the others were simply provided for through their connection.

It has been fine all my life, but I was sixteen now and would be required to start participating in the unity ceremonies. This by itself was no big deal as I was very good at faking my connection by now and the others weren't really capable of thinking that one of us might not be connected to *the whole*. But now... The See'r was coming, and they called them See'rs for good reason. I was worried.

Aaron's voice brought me back. "What do you think she looks like?" he asked over his shoulder.

"The See'r?" I called back.

"Of course, the See'r, you dork. Who else would I be talking about?" he said.

"I don't know," I told him, "probably really shriveled up like a raisin. She's going to be three hundred years old in a couple of days. Even the elders aren't that old, and look at how well they get around." I took the water bag from him.

He had stopped by the stream that ran to the river that eventually ended in the ocean and we both sat down in the grass beside the water. I took a big drink and handed the bag to him. He took another swig, replaced the cap, and put the bag into his backpack. He looked at me and said, "I bet she has to use two canes."

He grinned and threw a rock in the stream. It skittered along the water's surface and hit the far bank before ricocheting into the underbrush. That was my cue to start walking again. I stood and reached out my hand to pull Aaron to his feet. With a hefty tug, he was standing, and we headed back to the path that led to the Sacred Cave.

Aaron did most of the talking the rest of the way. He had recently taken notice of a girl from a nearby village, and he was prone to talk about her nonstop.

With the excitement of the morning, he hadn't mentioned her yet that day, so he began making up for lost time as he told me the newest information about her. Her name was Margie, she was fifteen, and she had three older brothers. She was of the Hill Folk who lived in a village of dugout homes about twenty miles north of The Birth Tree. The Hill Folk were people who found their connection to *the whole* to be more in tune with the soil, and they chose to commune accordingly. There were also Water People and Sky People, who each connected in their own ways to the various elements of *the whole*. Neither Aaron nor I had ever met any other Hill Folk, but the lore told of complete unification long ago.

When the Renaissance first took place, the Thirty had each been attuned to all that *the whole* was made of. But over time, humans began to develop their own ways of being. They started to only be able to commune in certain manners, and humans began grouping accordingly. To each their own.

"… and so I think ultimately that I'll just have to go to her village and ask her to a party. Of course, we'll have to *throw* a party in order for that to happen," he said, unaware that I was barely paying attention as we walked along.

Aaron looked to me hopefully. He was asking if we could have a party at The Tree, and he knew I would eventually say yes if he pestered me long enough.

"Won't she be here tomorrow for the celebration?" I asked. "I can almost guarantee it with Maggie attending. It won't be long before the whole forest is here to see her. Can't you talk to Margie then?" I asked Aaron.

"Yeah," he told me, "I thought of that, and while I might be able to find her in all the excitement, it won't be for sure, and I can't plan out the circumstances like I would be able to at your place…hint hint." He gave me a soft jab with his elbow in the ribs for added effect.

"I don't know… The elders did *not* like us using The Birth Tree for that game night a few weeks ago. Do you really think that they would let us throw an actual party there?" I said.

"No…" Aaron said, and he furrowed his brow. I could see his thinking process play out on his face and soon he was smiling again.

"We could have it at the pond! The elders won't be able to say anything about us using the pond, it's a public space! And people can just use the bathrooms at The Tree like they do for town meetings," he said.

"I think you better think this all through while we're getting the cave ready, and then see if you can find her at tomorrow's celebration," I said. "Who knows what will happen with Maggie here…?" I drifted off as I thought about my future.

The path rounded a corner and the forest gave way to a meadow that was dotted with wild rose bushes. The path wandered through the branches of multihued petals and thorns, and at the end, we could see the looming opening of the Sacred Cave. The roses were somewhat overgrown and we had to turn sideways in places in order to get through with our clothing intact.

We picked our way through the fallen rocks that had eroded from the mound that housed the cave. We could smell the dampness as we got closer, and we stood at the mouth of the cavern before going in.

"ECHOOO!" Aaron yelled, startling me and making me jump, but his word came right back to us in reverberation, deep from the very reaches of the cave. We turned and looked at each other, wide-eyed at the sound. The acoustics were incredible!

"If you're going to throw a party, you should do it here," I told him.

Aaron flashed me a smile that shone big and bright against the backdrop of the cave. He turned back to the darkness and said, "My dear friend, I was just thinking the exact same thing."

We set our bags down against a large boulder just inside of the entrance. We walked single file through the winding walkway that branched off in different directions leading to the various sections of the great rift. Our eyes adjusted to the low level of light, and we began to see the details of the cave.

We could see the large hearth whose fires had blackened the cave walls behind it. We could see the different sleeping areas that lay scattered throughout the rocky floor, and the old cloth sheets that covered mattresses of dried grasses.

We found the small stream that poured out of the rock at the end of the cave before disappearing again into the bowels of the earth. It was like this small part of this water's journey was strictly reserved for the animals of *the whole*. Humans and fauna alike would all stop here along their journeys, and Aaron and I too drank deeply from the stream before going on about our work.

Everywhere we could see, in every nook and cranny that would hold even the smallest of candles, there were heaps of melted wax. These were the remains of the recognition offered to the cave by the people for its role that it played in the salvation of humanity. Lore told that a single candle burning and wax dripping down through the night was what had triggered the search for new reading material, ultimately starting the braids of events that led to our new state of evolution. These types of candle offerings were most appropriate.

"I'll start clearing out all of the debris and you get a fire started so we can light some more offering candles. We don't know when she'll be here, so we need to light the big ones so they'll stay lit through the night," I instructed Aaron.

I began removing the wayward bits of rubble that had sloughed off the cave walls over the years, and Aaron moved to the charred pit. I watched him briefly as he knelt down and communed with *the whole*.

He didn't ask for fire, like I had to do. Aaron was able to connect to our entirety and he formed the fire through his connection. The pit sprung to life at his touch, and I shook my head at him and went back to picking up rocks.

I gathered up the old sleeping rolls and dumped them on the fire. The grasses and weathered cloth caught immediately, and the cave was bathed in the orange glow and warmth of sacred firelight.

Aaron joined me as I gathered fresh dried grasses to compile a new bed for the See'r. The grass was still warm from the sun as I carried the bundle up from the meadow, and I could smell the stalks' clean and earthy aroma as I heaped them in a pile on the bed-space closest to the fire. I walked on them a bit to flatten them, and then again when Aaron brought up his armload. When we had enough to ensure a nice soft space for Maggie, I covered the grasses in the new sheets we had packed. Hopefully it would be enough for the old See'r.

Our shadows danced across the cave walls as Aaron and I went around, each with a burning stick, igniting the remaining candles that sputtered and hissed before catching fire.

Aaron could have just made them light, but it was generally considered overindulgent to use *the whole* for simple tasks that were easily done in the regular fashion, a big reason I've been able to remain undiscovered. When the candles had been lit, we stood back and admired our work.

The cave was almost inviting now, quaint even. The fire danced with the breeze in its pit . Hundreds of burning wicks projected the silhouettes of sharp, rocky edges so that layers of shadow comingled across the ceiling. And as I tossed an armful of fresh pine needles onto the fire, the cave filled with a cleansing smoke and aroma that purged the final mustiness from the sacred place. I held my arm up and Aaron slapped my palm in a congratulatory high five. The sound bounced around the walls.

"I guess that's it for the day, eh?" he asked me as he stooped to pick up his bag. He opened it and produced the bread we had gotten from his mom, and he split it in two. He handed me half and then took a large bite out of his piece.

I started to nibble at mine, and Aaron began chatting away again about Margie through huge mouthfuls of half-chewed dough. We had only walked for about ten minutes when Aaron's romantic monologue was interrupted. "… two to three kids is probably the best number, but I know that the Hill Folk tend to have a few more kids than others, and so…" He stopped.

Above the birds and their songs, above the rustling of the forest leaves and the clacking of branches in the wind, we heard something new.

We paused in our tracks along the path. Aaron and I looked at each other to make sure we'd both heard it. Over the sounds of the forest was a whirr. A steady vibration grew louder as we stood there peering through the trees. As it got closer, we realized the sound was coming from above the trees, that it was coming from the sky.

Aaron and I scrambled for the clearing we knew was close by and we quickly scaled the large rock that protruded from the ground along the clearing's edge. We climbed as high as we could, keeping our balance, and we looked out far above the ocean of treetops.

In the distance, we could see what looked like three large dragonflies flying directly towards us. They were making the humming noise, and as they drew nearer and the buzz grew more intense, Aaron and I were soon able to make out the riders who sat on the backs of the great flying objects: three riders on two, and four riders on one.

"Sky Folk!" we said at the same time. They flew closer and we could make out the different parts of the aerial machines as the metal shone in the sunlight. They didn't really resemble dragonflies when you got a good look at them, but their interworking parts were a sight to behold. Being Tree Folk, Aaron and I had learned that machines would work in unison with *the whole*, and even help to progress it, but we had never seen anything like this before in our lives.

The three machines turned as they neared our spot, and Aaron and I dove for cover among the trees as they started circling the cave where we had just been.

Hidden under the canopy, we watched through leafy windows as two of the machines began to hover in place above the Sacred Cave and the craft with the four riders slowly descended to the meadow floor. We had walked about half a mile before we stopped, and we could hear the noise from the third flyer quieting as it landed. She was here! The See'r was here! Aaron and I looked at each other with relief; she had almost caught us! It was one thing to help set up the place; it was quite another to have to come face-to-face with an actual member of the Thirty, essentially the most famous person in the world now that the others were gone.

"Looks like we got outta there just in time," I said as I slid down the rock and hit the dirt with a thud. Aaron followed and grabbed our packs. We had to get back and tell the village the See'r had arrived.

"Yeah," Aaron said, "it would have been creepy to meet her all by ourselves." We tightened our bag straps and started to run back down the path towards the village.

*

We arrived home out of breath. We had run nonstop from the clearing and took the creek shortcut where we had to rock-jump down the stream. This is something Aaron and I did for fun, so we were good at it and good at avoiding getting wet. We collapsed in a tangled mess at the foot of the announcement rock, and we drank heavily from the water bag before we attempted to sound the call. We coughed and wheezed as the water poured in and around our mouths, but we drank until the bag was empty.

Finally able to catch our breaths, Aaron was first to stand, and he held out his hand to help me up. I took it, and he yanked me up to standing. We clambered up onto the announcement rock and began to shout.

"She's here! She's here!" I yelled, as Aaron shouted, "We saw the Sky Folk bring her! We saw Sky Folk!"

One by one, people started coming out of their tree-homes. Before long, they began taking up the chant. "She's here!" they cried. The elders showed up shortly after and shooed Aaron and I off the rock. Silence swept over the village as the senior elder took his spot on the leadership rock.

"People of the village," he began, "the younglings speak truth! We the elders have indeed felt the See'r arriving through *the whole*, and we will send out a welcome party to retrieve her for the opening unification ceremony tonight!"

A loud cheer went up from the crowd and people began to raise their hands to volunteer their services. Aaron was about to raise his hand before I stopped him with a hiss. "What are you doing, dude? I'm not going back there again tonight; we just got back."

"OK, fine," he said, "then we need to make sure we get good seats for the ceremony."

"Fine," I said, "but I'm going to go rest a bit and change clothes before we go. We can meet up on the bench out front just after sunset." Aaron agreed, and we parted ways.

I went into my room and asked the shower to turn on. The water instantly grew hot as its path was rerouted closer to the underground thermal pockets, and I took off my clothes and stepped in as the steam began to fill the polished living shower. I washed away the sacred grime that had accumulated during the cleaning, and I worried. The See'r had arrived in time for the ceremony, and I hadn't a clue as to what I was going to do about my secret. Surely, she would be able to see right through me to my disconnection. Maggie had been alive for three hundred years and had presumably lived her life within the very innerworkings of *the whole*. She could sense an outsider.

I asked the shower to shut off and I stepped out and reached for my towel. "Wait a minute," I said aloud, "maybe my way out of this has to do with her age..."

After three hundred years, time had to have dulled her awareness and her See'r abilities. She couldn't have gotten stronger after all that time, not when the others have all been dying off, I concluded. So, I could only really rely on her being feeble and unawares. She would expose me if I wasn't very careful.

*

Back in the main part of my room, I dressed again in my festive shirt. The villagers would be adorned in the most colorful things they owned, and the shirt would help me blend in.

I looked at myself one last time in the reflecting pool as I passed by, and I nodded at what I saw. I was just another townsfolk.

The courtyard in front of The Tree was a completely different place. There were natural lanterns made of vine and bioluminescence that had grown up around the perimeter of The Tree's trunk. These provided a green tinge to all of the activity that was taking place. Everywhere you looked, people were milling about, carrying trays of steaming foods and decorations. Live passion flowers had grown like streamers and the petal-studded vines crowned the entire affair in a ring of natural glory.

Long tables had been grown to accommodate the expected large crowds, and when urged on by the unity of the village, the tables themselves were producing the eating utensils for hundreds of hungry guests and townsfolk alike.

I took my place on the bench by The Tree and watched as I waited for Aaron to return.

The elders were back, and they were attempting to direct the action, but they went unheard as they struggled to be louder than everyone in the village talking to each other. They didn't need instruction anyways. I watched as each of their paths and actions intertwined with everyone else's. One person would spin around another, only to find someone else in their way, and they would raise up whatever it was they were holding so that the new person could pass underneath. This was taking place with each individual, flawlessly, before me. Each was in complete synchronization with one another, and each in complete symbiosis with *the whole*. It was as though they were performing a choreographed dance they all knew by heart.

My emotions grew and I felt my eyes start to get misty. I loved it here, and I loved the people. They had taken me in after my parents died, and they had loved me as one entity, as one of their own. These people were my family, and I felt like I had betrayed them all these years. I was not like them. I had never been like them, and I didn't think I ever could be. I was the flaw in *the whole*.

I saw Aaron dancing his own dance through the people as he headed my way, and I wiped my eyes. Once he was free of the throng, Aaron bounded up the steps to me, his glee infectious. I grinned at my best friend as he snagged a hat from a passerby and propped it crookedly atop his head.

The man protested, but his hands were full, and Aaron flashed a smile and said, "Merry Renaissance, my good fellow!" The man shook his head and carried on. Aaron plopped himself down on the bench next to me and wrapped his left arm around my shoulders. "Atty, me ol' boy," he said, "tonight will be a night to remember forever! Look at this." He gestured with his other arm at the preparations continuing in front of us. "Have you ever seen the village so alive?" He hugged me and I hugged him back. We smiled together at our village.

*

We saw the torchlights first as they began appearing between the trees. A single-file line of small, glowing embers told the village that the welcome party and the See'r had arrived.

Aaron and I stood on the bench for a better view. The lights grew brighter, and we started to see the human figures holding them as they arrived at the edge of the village. First, a few of the younger elders led the way. Next came random villagers who had gone along for fun, and then, we saw a hooded figure easily walking the path as it entered the realm of the Tree Folk.

Aaron spoke. "She sure doesn't walk like she's three hundred years old." I looked at him and nodded, my stomach beginning to tie itself into knots. This would not do. I had to get away from here, from Maggie. But I had to see her first. I would stick around long enough to at least see what she looked like, and then I would go to my room for the night. I could close up the windows and I wouldn't have to hear the revelry going on outside.

The group was just arriving at the announcement stone when the senior elder signaled for silence. The murmurs of the villagers quieted and the elder began to speak. "Tree Folk and other Folk alike," he said, waving his arm across the gathering, and sure enough, there were many more people present than just those from our village.

"We would like to welcome to our small part of *the whole*, to our tiny paradise, the very last survivor of the Thirty, the Great See'r and diviner, Maggie. The very last of the Cave Folk, and forever a part of all. We humbly ask you for your blessing."

At this, the hooded figure walked onto the rock and thanked the senior elder by placing her hands in his and bowing to him. As she bowed, I noticed a small gold chain with a charm fall from her neckline and spin back and forth, glinting in the torchlight. She turned to her audience and she reached up to remove her hood. She gently pulled back the green embroidered cloth from her head to reveal long silvery flowing hair.

Aaron and I stood on the bench, our mouths agape. We were bewildered by the beauty of the woman standing on the rock as she faced the gathered people.

She looked to be no more than forty years old. Nowhere near the three hundred that she actually was. She moved with a grace that put the dance of preparation to shame, and now I was getting worried that she would have no problem picking me out. She smiled and spoke; her voice was both powerful enough for all to hear, but also clean and clear, like a single bell ringing out in the night.

"Thank you all very much for having me to your village, and for letting me dwell in the Sacred Cave where the new world began. I can feel your unity and love surging through Us." She paused for the applause to subside before continuing.

"I come now to you, in celebration of the Renaissance that I had the privilege of witnessing, so that we may all rejoice in the lives that we live through the balance and the unity that was given to Us by our wisest of entities. The Being, Earth's true human form, had struggled for an eternity against humanity's ways of error, and endlessly pursued its given mission, when *the whole* felt itself reaching its breaking point.

"Time and time again, our Being changed lives. These lives fit together like the pieces of a puzzle, unbeknownst to The Being, until the puzzle was finally whole. A path to victory was granted. With its last lives in human form, our Being altered the life of a boy named Nathan in a way that would ensure he would one day become a law-changing Senator. It changed the life of a bus driver, who lost his daughter to racial violence, and whose voice sparked activism and protests across the country. Backed by Nathan, these protests enabled one of the world's first zero tolerance laws for racial radicalism. It saved a mother from spousal abuse, and that mother fully gave herself to the Being's mission, so that it may in turn save us all. Finally, the Being became a mute little girl. She was the last of its necessary forms, and the last of its endless struggle against hateful dogma. She was me. I was the Being's first bringer of light.

"Each of its ultimate physical embodiments were the stepping-stones of a past world that allowed our Being to bring about the necessary change for Us to live in perfect balance with *the whole*.

"Humans used to be taught to fight against *the whole* and to resist any progress that they themselves did not create. The powerful shackled the weak, and the weak were forced to abide by the structures in place, or cease to exist." She let this sink in for a moment before continuing.

"Renaissance Day is not just a day to celebrate what we have now. It is a day to celebrate that to which we never wish to return. It is a day to remember the name of Jacob, and a day to remember the name of Tiffany. A day to remember all of those who aided our Being with the grand struggle. Let us now join together with *the whole*, and each other, just as I joined as a young child with our great Being. Let us come together in unity for the opening ceremony." She bowed her head and hundreds of people joined her.

I watched as they all lowered their heads and reached out to *the whole* as one. I quickly bowed my head and tried to reach out along with them. I so wanted to be like everyone else, I just wanted to be normal, and I made one of the greatest efforts I had ever made.

I reached out to the singing crickets and the hooting owls. I reached out to the treetops and I reached out to the budding flowers. I could hear them. I was aware of their presence, but I could not *feel* them as much as I strained to do so. I was a failure, an abomination.

*

I wanted to feel, and feel is what I did. All of a sudden, I felt overcome with the energy of someone else in my space, in my very being. The energy forced my head up and my eyes open, and I found that I was staring directly into the dark eyes of the See'r. She had See'n me…

I tried to tear my gaze away from Maggie's deep pools of swirling energy, but I was firmly locked in place. She stared inside me, and left nothing unseen. She gripped my very soul. I was paralyzed while she examined me and I was only freed when she let me go to further address the crowd. I folded like a leaf in a fire and collapsed on the bench.

Aaron had missed the whole ordeal, with his own unity taking place, and so he grew alarmed when I fell down in a heap beside him. "Atty! Atty? Atty, are you OK? Are you OK, Atty?" He leaned over me and shook me.

"It…" I started. "It… It was just so beautiful," I told him as I managed to pretend to sob because of the ceremony.

"I felt it too, my friend, and it *was* beautiful!" he said, hugging me. I eased the charade of my crying and I let him help me to my feet. "Let's go get some food," my friend said, and I let him drag me to some open seats.

*

I couldn't eat. There were huge mounds of delicious food being passed under my nose and I didn't have an appetite for any of it. Aaron, next to me, made loud slurping and gobbling sounds as he wolfed down whatever tender morsels came his way. I could still feel her, and every time I looked in her direction, I could feel her attention turn back to me. Not the all-inclusive stare like the first time, but it was like she could feel me looking at her, and she knew whenever I did it.

I sat there for an hour, surrounded by celebration and cheer, unable to enjoy any of it. I watched as the village surrendered itself to indulgence and merriment under the unified essence of one of the See'r, and I felt sick.

Nobody noticed, not even Aaron, when I excused myself and dashed away from the table. The sound of laughter was soon far behind me as I lurched around to the back of The Tree. My stomach groaned in protest as I stumbled to the edge of my kitchen. I threw up in the hyacinth bush. Throwing up was something that happened very rarely around here. I was scared. What had the See'r done to me?

When my stomach had totally emptied itself, I pulled myself up from the bushes. I started to sweat as I stood, and then I was hit with chills as the night air blew across my exposed skin. I began shaking as I attempted to get back to my room, and I had to lean against the wall for support.

I could hear the raucous laughter as I finally made it to my room. I tore off my sweaty party shirt and kicked off my shoes. The world was swirling in front of me as I reached my bed and lay down in my moss. I pulled the tightly woven blanket over me, and was barely able to reach up to the wall to ask the windows to close. I vowed to run away in the morning. But not before I visited Maggie in the cave on my way out. I needed some answers.

*

I dreamt of my parents. It was so very real. I didn't dream of them dying, or of their death service, but of the fun that we used to have as a family. Visions upon visions sped past, and I saw us running through the forest playing hide-and-seek in the trees. I looked on as we picnicked by the pond, and as we danced in Renaissance happiness. I watched my entire childhood unfold in front of my sleeping eyes.

The visions slowed and they settled on a day where Mom, Dad, and I stood in the middle of the village after a day of honey gathering. It had been another time filled with family closeness and fun, and we had stopped in the courtyard for a moment to adjust our loads. Dad was helping Mom with her satchel, when he stopped, looked her in the eye, and kissed her. She kissed him back, and I ran over to hug their legs so as not to be left out. We stood there, the three of us hugging, unified in our little family.

I could feel their embrace as I slept. Then, in the dream, my parents gave me one last squeeze, before they turned back into the dust that makes up us all. Bits of Mom and Dad floated away as if windblown, and the bits started to cling to all that surrounded us. I watched as they clung to the trees and became one with them. I watched as they embodied the flowers and made them grow stronger. I watched as Mom and Dad disappeared again from my life, but I knew they were always with me.

*

I awoke with a start. Looking across the room to my small alarm peephole, I could see that it was still dark outside. Stars were shining between the branches, so it wasn't yet morning. I had to get up.

Something called to me. Something was pulling at my being. I could feel a great need to follow this "voice" that seemed to be beckoning me from my home. I got out of bed and dressed. I had an idea about what was happening, but after the dreams about my family, I wasn't sure. Maybe this was an opportunity to be able to see them again?

My stomach had returned to its usual self, and it grumbled out of hunger as I used the bathroom before leaving. I went by the kitchen and grabbed a banana as I passed through to head back to The Tree. I didn't want anybody to see me should there be any partiers remaining about.

The calling seemed to be coming from the direction of the pond. My sandals left footprints in the dew as it glinted off the grass in the moonlight. I ate my banana as I walked and my stomach settled. I neared the pond and marveled at the pristine reflection of the treetops and moon in its surface before I saw her.

Maggie sat on a rock that jutted out into the pond. Kids would jump off that very spot in splash competitions, but now it seemed a much more somber place in the presence of the See'r. Her hood was down again and her long silver hair shone in the moonlight as she sat cross-legged at the water's edge. She stared off into the distance across the pond, and she didn't turn at my approach. "Thank you for coming, Atticus," she said.

"Well," I whispered, "I didn't feel as though I had much choice in the matter, so here I am." She knew I was joking, and her laughed skipped across the water as she turned to face me. "Your humor bodes well for you so far," she said. "I am glad you keep it alive." Her eyes twinkled, a vast difference from the black-hole suns I had seen during the ceremony. "Come, sit with me. We have things to talk about."

I felt no nervousness when I bent down to sit next to a three-hundred-year-old See'r. I was completely at ease as I crossed my legs beside her and we stared out at the water together. After a few minutes of silence, I picked up a good skipping stone and hurled it across the pond. It flittered along the surface, leaving its impressions clear along the still waters. We both watched the concentric circles spread until they reached the edge of the pond and then bounced back onto themselves.

"Did you send me the dreams of my parents?" I finally blurted out. Maggie reached out and patted my leg, and her touch left an energy that felt as if moths were floating up my spine.

"No," she said, "not exactly. I sent you a connection to *the whole*, and you interpreted it as your mind deemed fit. You saw your parents because they were your strongest link to the rest of Us."

"How did you know that I didn't have a connection to *the whole*?" I asked.

"I could see you, of course. Or, I could *not* see you, rather," she told me. "When we came together for the ceremony, I could see *the whole* flowing freely through everyone and everything around us, but where you stood on that bench with your friend, I saw only a void. A blind spot where I would normally see the inner workings, I saw nothing. A shadow shaped of your own likeness. You are the first disconnected human in hundreds of years."

We were both silenced by her words. A faint glow started to appear in the east, and ripples from the morning insects began to dot the pond as we sat. Maggie was the first to interrupt our contemplation.

"This is not to say that you are not just as much of a part of *the whole* as anybody else, because you are, indubitably," she assured me. "You are simply unable to connect in the same way others do."

This was helpful to hear, and I was glad that I wasn't a complete defect. I had been feeling even more alienated lately, but sitting on that rock with Maggie, I found my worries to be gone.

"You must find other ways, your own personal ways, in which you feel the most comfortable communing with *the whole*," she said. "Where all other people can simply reach out and tap into the energy that makes up all of us, you must make your own connections. You will see these connections in the wind blowing autumn leaves from the treetops. You will see these connections when you see children playing. You will see them, if you look. Connections are witnessed in the love of family and friends, and connections are felt through the beating of our hearts. Connections are seen through the balance of *the whole*."

Maggie stopped and cocked her head to one side as if listening for something far off. Her hand shot up to her neck to grasp at her necklace. She seemed to frown, though it was hard to tell in the early morning light. She rubbed the golden trinket with her fingers. But the frown only lasted for a second before she nodded her silver head and continued.

"Three hundred years ago, every action had a relative *re*action. A push from one side was a pull from the other. This was the struggle that plagued humanity, and Us, for millions of years. It was not until we were shown by our Being that we had to cease fighting against the natural world and join it that it stopped. That the only way to win the internal human war, is to give in to the powers that created us in the first place. The flower produces seed, the bird eats the seed. The seed fuels the bird, and the bird spreads the seed. Water to vapor, vapor to water. Humans strove to stand in the way of these natural processes, and they handicapped them, more and more over time.

"Humans hoarded the energy others of the Us needed to survive, and gave nothing back. They gathered so much energy and power that they almost snuffed out the Earth entirely. As the old humanity unleashed all of its stolen energy, the force scorched everything it touched. But the energy was returned to *the whole*, and then it was applied back where it belonged. All energy is our energy; it only changes form. As you can see, you can connect to it as well."

The orange glow of sunrise was growing brighter by the minute. I inhaled deeply with every breath. I could smell the plants that lined the pond. The cattails were nourished by the fish-waste from the fish eating the insects. The insects sheltered and mated in the cattail, and their young hid in its roots.

The entire world was filled with these endless cycles of life that worked in symbiosis with one another to maintain the world's existence. Maggie began speaking again, as the frogs started to wake and offer their warming-up croaks.

"Each minute particle is just as important as the next fully formed being. Everything plays its part. Each human is no different than the being of salvation itself; this was so even before the great war. Each person, connected or not, has the potential to live their best life through complete compassion and love for every single part of *the whole*. All they need to do is make a conscious effort to reach out and ensure that connection is made and maintained. They must surrender themselves to the natural flow of energy that is already established in *the whole*.

"All people do this now, even you, but that will not be the case for much longer. You, Atticus, will need to be the example for all to come." Her cloak shifted as Maggie pointed a long finger at me. "You will have to find your connections to *the whole* and keep them pure. You, Atticus, will have to force yourself to exemplify the teachings of kindness and empathy that all others come to naturally in their connections."

I began to feel worried. The conversation had taken a dark turn and the tempo had changed after Maggie listened to the wind. It went from we and us to me, me, me, right after she had read *the whole*.

"What changed?" I asked the See'r. "Something is different now, and if it involves me, I think I have a right to know about it. Why am I like this?" I demanded.

Maggie locked eyes with me. For a short moment, I was at her mercy, but she immediately let me loose and looked down at her lap with a nod.

"If time is like a wheel," Maggie said, though her pace had quickened, "then you, Atticus, are the start of a new revolution. You are the rebirth of *the whole's* inevitable cycle." She slowed then and looked deeply into my soul as she told me, "You are the first ray of dawn; others will follow. Your disconnect is the beginning of the end."

When she said the word "disconnect," a huge gasp came from behind us. Maggie didn't turn to look, as though she knew who was there, but my head swiveled immediately at the noise.

Aaron had his backpack slung across one shoulder, ready to go draw the birth of the sun. He wore his favorite brown pants and a light gray jacket in defense of the morning briskness. Even his hair was askew like normal. But Aaron wore one thing I had never seen on him before: a look of pure fear.

I had seen this look on my parents' faces as they pushed me out of harm's way and then they turned to face the boulder. Their fear was the last thing I saw before I lost consciousness after I fell. I awoke with their faces burned into my mind, only to find that their final act in life had been to save mine.

Here, Aaron's face was distorted by emotion, but fear remained ever present as he processed what he had just heard. His best friend since childhood had always been disconnected from *the whole*, and he was ushering in a new dawn of change. People fear change.

I jumped up and tried to tell him to wait, to come sit and talk with us, but Aaron ran. I called his name, but he didn't turn back.

I put my hand on the old See'r's shoulder and I made her face me. "What is going to happen now? You're the See'r, tell me!" I begged.

Maggie sighed. "I cannot see the future, I can only see the now. I get messages from *the whole*, but mostly I don't know what they mean. Just hints here and there. But while we were talking, I got a very unambiguous push. This is the way. The cycle will play as it always has, and you will do your part. A new world order is afoot."

Maggie got up from the rock and began to walk away. "So now you're leaving too?" I yelled in desperation.

She turned around, nodded, and then took the steps back to me. She knelt down and removed her necklace. She took my hand and dropped the chain into it. I now had a good look at the charm that Maggie so revered. It was the letter *t*. "A cross, or crucifix. It might bring you peace, as it has me," Maggie told me before going on. "Atticus, remember the teachings that have brought us to this point in time. Exude love and compassion, even for those that will judge you harshly. Use your connections to *the whole* that you see, and maintain the balance and unity that has now been marred."

And with that, the great See'r, the last of the Thirty beings touched by the light, Maggie, the three-hundred-year-old child of *the whole*, broke into millions of tiny glimmering particles that went skipping about, finding brand-new things to become.

*

I was frozen in place. The past few hours had been a whirlwind of information and emotion. I wanted to run away. I wanted to crawl into bed. I wanted answers, but I had no way to get them. I was alone again, truly alone.

I didn't want to face the village, not yet. I had to see if I could get some more information from somewhere, but I didn't know who to turn to. My mind reeled with options when a bold and precise picture of the Sacred Cave came to me. I couldn't shake it. *Why would I go to the cave?* I tried thinking of other possibilities, but all that came up was Cave, Cave, Cave. I knew where I was headed.

I jogged around the far side of the pond, before circling back through the forest to pick up the trail that led to the cave. Here, I flat-out ran. The sun was fully above the horizon now, and its light pointed me deeper into the valley towards the cave. In no time I was running through the clearing where Aaron and I had seen the Sky Folk, and soon I could see candlelight flickering in the cave's recesses against the dark backdrop of the shadowed mountain. I slowed as I drew nearer, and began to walk. I wasn't sure if anybody was still there and I didn't wish to surprise them unnecessarily.

I called out as I walked through the rocks but all that came back was a faint echo. The larger candles were still burning, and the hearth still felt warm. Maggie's bedroll was there, and it looked untouched. She hadn't slept there the night before.

I went to the back of the cave and got a drink from the stream. I drank heavily as I realized how much the run had taken out of me.

I walked back to the hearth and sat down on the bed that I had made the day before. I crossed my legs and stared into the dark pile of ashes. I still didn't know what to do. The whole village would know by now, and I'm sure they would look at me differently. Hopefully, Aaron would talk to me again at some point.

I didn't ask for this. I didn't ask for my parents to die either. I just wanted to live my life. Is this how the great being felt for its entire struggle to save *the whole*? Did it constantly feel the deep empty pit of despair that I did? "Why did it have to be me?" I screamed into the cave. As the echo rang throughout the void in the mountain, I flung myself onto the grass-bed to muffle my sobbing.

My self-pity was short lived. In my desperation, I failed to notice the small circular object mostly hidden beneath the sheet.

It found me, though. As I tried to bury my face, it jabbed an edge right into the middle of my forehead. I saw stars, blinded by pain, and I rolled over onto my back as I held my bleeding head.

When the pain had eased a bit and I was able to think again, I dabbed at the wound using my shirtsleeve until I got the bleeding to stop. The wound wasn't that bad after all, but it did hurt. I turned to the thing underneath the sheet. The smell of freshly dried grass hit me as I pulled back the cover.

It looked like a coin at first. We would sometimes find old remnants of the world's past lives in the ground, and the elders had a bag of coins they would show us kids from time to time.

But as I leaned in, I noticed that the edge had small scallops in it. I had not seen a coin like this before. Plus, it showed no signs of ever being in the dirt. It glinted in the candlelight, and I could see the workings of a pin mechanism on the back. It was a brooch. It had to have been Maggie's. I picked up the silvery treasure.

*

Lightning flashed before my eyes as I touched the pin. My hand clenched tightly around the tiny circlet as an endless stream of *the whole* whirred through my head. I watched the most epic wars the world had ever known, and I saw the making of the continents. I joined the oceans in their tidal tango, and I roiled and churned with the molten core of *the whole*. I got to see every single wedding that had ever taken place, and I paid homage to every single death. I watched the great grid of energy in its constant ebb and flow, the heart of *the whole*, beating its matrix of infinite comingling life cycles. I was connected.

As soon as my personal Renaissance had begun, it was over. One second, I didn't know, and the next, I knew. I was aware, but I was still very much a disconnect. I looked down at my fist and willed my clinging fingers to release their grip on the pin.

There were small indentations in my fingers and palm, just beginning to turn a purplish hue from bruising, but I knew they were a small price to pay. The tiny brooch was etched with a tree that looked similar to The Birth Tree, but on the brooch, the tree's branches were a rope tied in an endless knot. Maggie had to have left this for me.

But if so, why wasn't I connected? I possessed the knowledge of the eternal struggle: good versus evil. I had witnessed how everything of *the whole* connects and how all should be treated respectfully. Am I to go through life in this limbo between connected and not?

The brooch lay in my palm. It no longer shone in the light, and it seemed to be aging before my eyes. I stared at it as it started to corrode and crumble in my open hand. Bits began to fall off. Slowly at first, and then faster and faster as rot spread through it. The leaves appeared to fall from the silver tree as the metal signet disintegrated. Soon, there was nothing left of the tiny brooch but a pile of dust that was blown from my hand by a steady gust of wind. It had given me my answers, and it was gone. The bruised ring in my palm was all that was left.

I looked around the cave and I no longer felt its pull telling me I needed to be here. A breeze picked up. I could feel it swirl around me to reach further into the cave. It pushed against the flames of the candles, making them leap and dance in the darkness. Their shadows played tag on the ceiling as the breeze increased, and one by one, the candles were blown out, leaving me again alone in the void.

That's all I got. A brief, but powerful reminder of how all others are able to tap into the greatest known resource. I would never forget this, so perhaps that is all that I needed to move forward. I turned to walk the path that would take me to face the village.

*

I did not run back. I walked, meandered even, along the dirt path. I didn't know what I was going to say. I didn't know who to talk to first, and I didn't know what was going to happen to me. I had betrayed them all, especially Aaron, with my deceit. My hope was that they would rely on their connection to *the whole*, and to the sage teachings of our enlightened Being, and they would understand that I was no less a part of Us than the next person. I had to trust in *the whole* and the cycles of life.

I could hear the village before I saw it. The noise of hundreds of people talking all at once carries a long way, even in the forest. Their individual shouts were joined together into one single incoherent roar of unrest as I turned the last corner. Nobody saw me coming up the path. They were all focused on the elders who stood crammed together on the speaking rock trying to calm the frenzied mob.

I had never seen anything like it, nor had anyone else. This was not good. The entire village stood in the square, and everyone was demanding answers. I left the path and remained in the trees as I circled around them unnoticed. I could see the faces of my family as they yelled, and I could see what I had seen on Aaron's face earlier: fear. I was causing fear.

I had to leave and I had to go now. I couldn't let this happen. I couldn't let them fear me. I couldn't let them fear at all! Fear was the root of all evil.

I moved slowly through the trees around to the back of The Birth Tree. I moved silently through the flowering kitchen and down the oaken insides of my home. In my room, I pulled shirts and pants from their hangers in the closet, and I stuffed them into my backpack. I threw in some socks and my other pair of shoes, and then I looked around the room in which I had spent the majority of my life. The room looked smaller to me, like I had somehow grown in the past day, but I felt a larger connection to the home. I felt remorse as I went into the bathroom one final time.

I turned on the tap and let the sink fill with warm water. When the last drop fell, the water stilled to a calm. I could see myself in the reflection, and I could see the small vertical gash in my forehead from Maggie's brooch. Blood had dried around the cut, and I scooped the water into my hands and washed it away. The mark was still there, but at least I no longer looked as if I had been in an accident.

I took one final look at myself and then asked the water to drain. I would probably have a scar. I grabbed my bag from the moss-covered bed and put it on my shoulder. I raised my hands and placed them onto the soft wall of the living home. It had sheltered me and held me while I shed my childhood tears. It had provided and offered sustenance, and I thanked it for all that it had given me before turning and leaving my room.

I could still hear the village and I walked the halls to the front entrance so that I could proffer myself to them. Their fear was creating new ripples in *the whole*, and I had to try to stop them. I paused for a moment behind the big round door and took a deep breath.

"Whatever will be, will be," I told myself, and I opened the door.

The first view of me standing at the door with The Birth Tree towering behind me in all of its glory brought a silencing wave across the villagers. No one made a sound as I stepped out and peered into the faces of my family. The sound had stopped, but the expressions were the same. Each member of the village looked at me nervously.

They no longer saw me as the little boy they had all cared for over the years. They no longer saw me as one of their own. I was an outsider who had lied to them from the beginning. They no longer saw me as a part of *the whole*, but as a threat to it. I was something they had never encountered before, and they feared the unknown.

They parted as I walked towards them, shying away from me as if my very touch would damn them for eternity. I walked through my family, enduring their stares, and made my way slowly to the rock. The elders stumbled over each other as they tried to get away from me. I climbed up onto the empty rock and turned around for all to see.

I could feel the tension of their energy as it unified into a single collective focus of *the whole*. I felt them probing me. Not as intensely as Maggie had, but I could still feel it. They began to shrink back in horror as their probes came back empty, having reached my voided being, returning with nothing. I was the only negative being in a completely positive world.

Whispers began. Pointing and cringing. Mothers hid their children behind them. Fathers stepped forward to block them from me. The tension grew and I was at a complete loss for words that would ease it.

I saw Aaron. His height stood out easily among those who were shorter than him. He was not scared or pointing or whispering like the others. Aaron's face told a whole different story. He looked angry and betrayed. He looked down for a moment, like he was searching for something. When he lifted his head back up, he reached his right arm behind his head and flung his arm forward. Time slowed down as I watched the flat speckled river rock come flying in my direction.

I knew exactly what it was. Aaron was always on the lookout for the perfect skipping stone. Whenever he found one, he would stick it in his pocket for the next time.

My eyes welled with tears as I understood what was happening. The rock was closing the gap, and I didn't even have the will to move out of the way. Through my blurred vision, I watched it twist and turn through the air as I stood helpless. I felt responsible for this. This was my fault, and I would take what *the whole* doled out.

The stone hit me in the forehead with a horrible crunch. Right in the same spot as the brooch. My eyes filled with red as I sank to my knees. The sight of the stone hitting me was all it took to snap the tension. A sickening cheer rose up from my family as they rushed to the dais and began pummeling me with whatever they could find.

I could feel my bones breaking as they beat me with rocks, logs, and their fists. I didn't try to stop them. I watched my pain as it grew like a fire. I begged *the whole* for a new start, for a new beginning where I was connected, but it didn't listen. My family brutalized me to the brink of death.

As my body began convulsing and giving up its grip on life, I was able to force my hand to move. With my last scrap of strength, I placed my palm on the announcement rock, and I asked *the whole* to take me back into its ever-loving embrace.

*

A deep groaning overtook the bloodthirsty screams of murder. My family fell to their knees as the ground started to quake, and a deafening BOOM shook the village. I could hear the creaking and cracking of great timbers splitting, and the sadistic screams morphed into human cries of terror. My family ran as I lay there in the near-death state. They ran as The Birth Tree split in two and came crashing down upon the town square.

I felt a tremendous whoosh of air around me and I was covered in branches and leaves. I could sense the limbs brushing against me as they swayed from the force, but they didn't stop. The foliage began to grow. The leaves grew broader, and the branches elongated, and The Tree started wrapping itself around my bruised and broken body. I could feel myself being lifted from the rock.

The branches cradled me and the large covering leaves flooded my body with a tidal wave of warming love and compassion of a magnitude I had never known. My wounds stopped bleeding, and my bones began mending themselves. The branches gently carried my healing body to the trunk of the massive Tree.

The Tree lifted me into itself, and lovingly placed me into my moss-covered bed that remained undamaged inside. The walls around the bed started to grow, and soon The Tree was creaking and groaning. The living-wood squeaked as its broken pieces rubbed together and repaired its gaping wounds around me as I lay inside. Complete darkness closed in on me as I was swallowed and entombed in The Rebirth Tree.

A small voice spoke.
It said I was going to be fine…
"Here," it told me, "we have tacos."

*

"FUCKING MORONS!" I was wrenched from my slumber as soon as the rock was thrown at young Atty. I could feel the change in his friend Aaron, the precise moment when a piece of his light suddenly went dark. Atticus wasn't evil for being different; the evil came to fruition through the *treatment* of his difference, the human response to the unknown. Differences are not to be feared, but should be celebrated for the opportunities that they provide to gain knowledge.

The rebirth of evil was something I had feared would happen eventually, but I did not think that the cycle would be so short. Once we had purged the darkness from *the whole*, the balance was no longer true. There can be no good without evil, for if there is nothing to compare goodness to, the bar is perpetually out of reach.

A new evolutionary cycle is upon Us. *The whole* is changing once again, as it always has, since the very beginning. My hunger grows as I feel my energy gathering itself from the very reaches of *the whole*, and from my tree.

I know not who my newest host will be, but it will not be young Atticus. It can't be. Not only does the poor kid need a lot of rest, but he has a very different path ahead of him. He is the harbinger of darkness, a pariah of solitude in a world of unification. This new path cannot be stopped by me, or by any other. Even if I merged with him now, the seeds have already been planted. *The whole* will always strive for balance. Good *must* have evil to exist. Atticus *must* do his part.

Going forward, these ignorant assholes better listen.

And if they start getting rowdy again, I'll just come back as the water.

Like, all of it.

"I'm sorry that you're thirsty, lady, but you coughed on people in Walmart during a pandemic. Fuck off."

Come to think of it, maybe they should all just assume that everyone they meet is me. That would solve most of the evil that had previously been fostered, and actually cause people to respect one another.

A new era is dawning. One of rebalance, and one completely blind to foresight. Humanity has had their little hiatus; it's time for them to get back to work.

And of course, there will most <u>definitely</u> be tacos…

Made in the USA
Las Vegas, NV
01 August 2024

93213056R00118